MALMA STATION

MALMA STATION

ALEX SCHULMAN

Translated from the Swedish by Rachel Willson-Broyles

FLEET
2024

FLEET

Originally published in Sweden in 2022 by Albert Bonniers Förlag
First published in Great Britain in 2024 by Fleet

1 3 5 7 9 10 8 6 4 2

Copyright © 2022 by Alex Schulman
English translation copyright © 2024 by Rachel Willson-Broyles

The moral right of the author has been asserted.

A CIP catalogue record for this book
is available from the British Library.

Hardback ISBN 978-0-349-72801-8
Trade Paperback ISBN 978-0-349-72802-5

Typeset in Bembo by M Rules
Printed and bound in Great Britain by
Clays Ltd, Elcograf S.p.A.

Papers used by Fleet are from well-managed forests
and other responsible sources.

Fleet
An imprint of
Little, Brown Book Group
Carmelite House
50 Victoria Embankment
London EC4Y 0DZ

An Hachette UK Company
www.hachette.co.uk

www.littlebrown.co.uk

For Amanda

Chapter 1

Harriet

She stands in her father's shadow on the platform, watching as he squints into the low morning sun. They wait. She looks for signs of annoyance in his eyes or in the way he moves. She's especially attentive today because they're taking this journey on account of her, which makes her feel like she's indebted to him. It's because of her that Dad is standing there now. She endures the heat, endures the early morning, endures the delayed train; she takes responsibility for everything he must tolerate from now on, and he is silent and impossible to read.

The asphalt is hot, its warmth rising through the soles of her shoes. Harriet is dressed entirely in black, because that's what you do for funerals. She's carrying her father's camera bag over her shoulder and does not set it on the ground. Not even when she learns that the train is delayed, and they might be standing there for a while, does she let go of it. In that bag are accessories worth thousands of kronor. She knows the equipment is important to Dad. She also knows it's her future she's carrying over her shoulder, because one day she will inherit it all, and each time he tells her this it's as though a weight is placed upon her. Dad does camera care once a week, and he always wants her to take part. They sit under the orange glow of the kitchen light and he lines up the lenses on the kitchen table, and sometimes he hands her one so she can feel it. 'Look at this guy,' he says. And she feels its heft in her hand; the lens is huge and heavy, wants to hit the floor. 'And this one,' he says. He hands her another. 'Look at this guy.' Dad often calls various objects 'guys'. Especially ones he has bought and takes good care of, but other things too; in the car, for instance, he might suddenly stop to point if he spots a deer: 'Look at that guy.' A tree that has fallen in the woods can also be a guy, if it's a large tree. But most of the time, it's all about possessions – and not just ones that belong to him; he's also generous with praise for the belongings of others. In the car, he might whistle if he ends up behind a Porsche. 'Wouldja look at that guy.' It's a nice habit; in those moments, she likes her father.

Does Dad maybe want to sit down somewhere? She scans the area, but the benches are already full of people; they look silly, a row of craned necks anxiously searching for signs of a train that never comes. A conductor moves swiftly across the platform and someone asks what's going on, and the man simply points down the tracks, as if the answer were there in the distance, and he were on his way to find it. Then suddenly there's wild movement as a voice announces the train's arrival, and everyone's in such a hurry, as if they know for certain the train will only stop at the station very briefly. But Dad isn't in a rush. He never is. It's something about the way he moves, as though he does everything at half-speed. There is nothing that happens out of the blue, nothing done on impulse; Harriet gets the sense that everything is planned from the start. Sometimes she imagines that he decides every morning exactly how he will move throughout the day, from breakfast until night-time, and then he performs it all just as he'd pictured. Maybe that's why he never shows any emotion, because nothing can ever surprise him, he's never at a loss to respond. Now he watches the people rushing to their train cars, he lets them do their thing, and then he slowly starts to walk and Harriet follows. It's just as hot inside the compartment as outside; she walks through the car and sees people sitting there feeling uncomfortable with themselves.

She sits down across from her father in a window seat. He gestures for her to hand over the camera bag, and she does. She looks out of the window at the slowly depopulating platform. The sounds around her get closer – the rustle of newspapers being unfolded, a carbonated bottle opening – and conversations begin to take shape, stumps of discussions. Once she's started listening she can't turn it off, and she catches everything because the conversations sound like faint hums that form melodies, stories about lives. And just about everyone she listens to seems sad and weighed down by an inexplicable heaviness. And all the while she's afraid of being confronted if someone notices her – why are you eavesdropping?

She's not supposed to eavesdrop.

She remembers the night two years ago when she and her sister were meant to be asleep, and the bedroom shared a wall with the kitchen, where Mom and Dad were. Every word was crystal clear. It was almost strange – could it have been that the wall between the kitchen and the girls' bedroom actually amplified sound? That must have been the case, because it was like she was right there with them and could hear the sighs, the scraping of chairs, the gentle rumbling of the fridge that stopped when Dad opened it. He stood there taking it in for a little too long. Mom didn't like members of the family to stand with the fridge door open, she didn't like the indecisiveness – 'Do something!' – and she was worried about their finances too; she had got it into her head that the electric bill was high because the fridge door was open all the time. And that's why she sometimes shouted: 'Don't stand there dilly-dallying – close that door!' But that night, Dad was able to stand at the fridge for a long time, looking at the possibilities all lined up inside, with no objections from Mom.

This pause caught Harriet's attention; something was off. Rustling paper, Dad took out a bit of ham, transferred something heavier to the counter – the tub of butter? He opened the freezer for ice cubes. Dad drank his milk with ice, it was a habit. Sharp sounds and clattering from the silverware drawer, as though someone were digging through a treasure chest full of gold. She heard Mom light the candles on the table and set out plates; it was quiet and it took a long time, and Harriet lay in bed listening to the ominous sounds as Mom and Dad sat down across from each other by the window.

'So how are we going to do this?' said Mom.

Dad didn't respond.

What was happening on the other side of the wall?

'Want some?' he asked. 'Thanks,' she replied.

The friendliness between them. Their soft voices between bites. The consideration, the almost exaggerated politeness. Would you like something to drink? I'll get it. They seemed to be getting along better than ever.

'I suppose you'll be moving up to live with him,' Dad said.

'Yes,' Mom replied. 'He's got a big place and there's room for kids there too.'

'You aren't taking both of them.'

'No,' said Mom. 'My suggestion is I take Amelia and you take Harriet.'

He barked out a laugh. 'I was going to suggest the opposite,' he said.

'You want Amelia?' Mom asked.

'Yes.'

And then both of them fell silent as they chewed their sandwiches. A glass was filled.

'Amelia and I are close,' said Mom. 'And we share our interest in riding.'

'Me too.'

'But you don't ride.'

'No, but Amelia and I are close.'

'Why don't you want to take Harriet?' Mom asked.

'Why don't you want to take her?'

'I asked you first,' said Mom.

Harriet lay in bed, staring at the ceiling.

'You know why,' Dad said. He drank his milk. 'I find Harriet tricky. We don't quite jibe.'

Harriet's bed was narrow and had high wooden edges, like a coffin without a lid. It had stopped raining and the storm had moved on, no more wind shaking the treetops in the park outside. She didn't hear anything now, just the sound of her parents eating in the kitchen, and their quiet conversation.

They don't quite jibe.

Later on, she'd always felt that this was so vague, so hard to put her finger on. What could she do to be better? She wanted them to jibe, but didn't understand how to make it happen.

She turned in the bed, towards her sister. 'Amelia,' she whispered. 'Did you hear that?'

Her sister didn't respond, but through the dim light Harriet could see she was wide awake, lying on her back with her eyes on the ceiling.

'Amelia.'

'They're talking a load of crap,' her sister whispered. 'Don't listen to them.'

Their parents didn't speak about it any further that night; the conversation must have continued elsewhere, and a few days later, in the afternoon, the sisters were called into the kitchen one at a time. Mom opened a can of cola and handed it to Harriet, even though it wasn't Saturday. It was warm and the bubbles grew in her throat as she drank. Her parents were wearing odd smiles. They were going to get a divorce, Mom said, and since they would be living far apart it was best to split up the kids and Harriet was going to live with Dad and Amelia was going to live with Mom. Harriet waited for Dad to say something, but he remained silent. She glanced up at him and saw his blank face and she felt sorry for her father, because he hadn't gotten what he wanted.

They're sitting across from each other next to the train window. Dad keeps looking over her head to keep an eye on the doors. She knows what he's waiting for, and she's pre-pared, they've gone through it step by step — when he gives the signal, they have to be quick. He opens the camera bag, which is in his lap. His eyes firmly on the door, he doesn't need to look down, he knows his camera bag inside and out. His glasses make his eyes smaller, two black dots behind the lenses. You can never tell what he's thinking.

She looks out of the window: they travel across bridges high above the water, the train is going fast, the flowers in the ditch alongside the tracks make a blurry blue stripe. They've left the city now and are passing suburbs, then farms and green fields, and she's riding backwards and watching people go by and shrink behind the train, their lives turning into tiny points that dissolve into the fields. Then the train slows down – and stops completely. A voice from the loudspeaker says that there is only a single track ahead of them and they have to wait for an oncoming train to pass. They're sunken into a meadow, flowers up to their chins. If the summer rises another few inches, they'll drown. A little further off in the field she can see two birds with long, skinny legs gazing out at the valley, and she happens to think of the time her dad showed her a squirrel he'd found in a tree. Look at that guy. The squirrel had completely stopped what it was doing and was looking out at the forest without moving a muscle. It was like it was paralysed, stuck in a thought. 'He's sitting there remembering,' Dad had said, and this had seemed to her like such a distressing idea, an unbearable one. Because it made the sorrow in the world greater; that heaviness was found not only in people but also in animals, and she had to be responsible for them as well. And now, as she watches the two birds in the field, she imagines that they're remembering something from their childhood, and it just makes her sad.

She received an assignment in school a few months ago, when they were learning about the brain. Each student was supposed to write down a memory, recounting as many details as possible. She'd told her dad about the assignment that evening, and it piqued his interest. 'So what memory are you going to write about?' he asked.

'I don't know, something that happened in my childhood.'

At that, Dad laughed and said, 'You're eight years old. You ARE a child.'

After that, she sat in her room with her notebook and wrote about the crucifix Dad had on the wall. It used to be over his desk, but after the divorce he hung it on the wall above his pillow. She's seen Dad fall to his knees beside the bed and clasp his hands and pray. When he's not in the room, she likes to get close and contemplate the cross: a dark-metal Jesus against the black-painted wood; the bundle around Jesus's waist, like a diaper; the big bolts that go through his palms, and one spike through his feet; one knee in front of the other, which makes him seem feminine somehow. God's son aims a steady gaze over the bedspread and when she stands right in front of the crucifix and looks at him, it seems as if he's looking back. Dad had told her it could take days for the crucified to die, sometimes a whole week, and when at last they did die it wasn't from their wounds but from thirst or starvation. Harriet wrote about this, and then she recounted a memory that was a year old, something that had happened right after the divorce. She was visiting her grandma, Dad's mom. Grandma had eczema on her hands and used potato flour to ease the itching; she always carried the flour around in a cloth bag, and Harriet remembered the dust that would whirl up in tiny, illuminated particles when the sun found its way in through the big windows. Sometimes Grandma would put on transparent plastic gloves and let the flour trickle into them over her wrists, adding more whenever it started itching again, and by the end of those evenings the flimsy gloves were always full, heavy with the white powder.

Grandma was afraid of death, preoccupied by it, and often sat in silence at the kitchen table, her face turned away. And sometimes when her fear of death became too great she would go to the piano and strike the keys full force, which made it seem like the whole world was crashing down. Then she lingered at the piano and squeezed her hands together hard, making the plastic gloves squeak.

Only alcohol could loosen her from this grip. She drank

9

fridge-chilled red wine, and after a few glasses she became chatty and started asking Harriet questions. Once Harriet told her that a friend had given her a snake bite at pre-school, and Grandma asked what a snake bite was, and she explained that it's when you twist the skin on someone's arm in opposite directions, like wringing a dishrag, and Grandma laughed. 'Show me,' she said, rolling up the sleeve of her silk blouse. And Harriet twisted her grandmother's skinny arm, and there was blood almost immediately. Grandma gave a shrill, loud shriek, and the blood kept coming, running down her arm, and she started looking through the cupboards for the first aid kit but couldn't find it anywhere. The cupboards opening and closing, Grandma's whimpering. 'Jesus Christ, child, help me look,' she said, but Harriet couldn't. She stood in the middle of the kitchen, paralysed, Grandma's blood on her hands. Dad had to come pick her up early, and when she got home that night she walked by Dad's room and there was the cross above the bed, and when she looked at Jesus she thought he was looking back at her in a new way.

She turned in the assignment and forgot about it, but one afternoon when she walked into her room, Dad was sitting at her desk and reading her notebook.

'Did you turn this in?' he asked.

'Yes,' she replied.

He kept reading as she stood before him in silence, and then he closed the notebook and looked at the floor. 'You have a good memory,' he said.

'Yes,' she replied.

'But listen. What happens in our home stays in our home.'

'OK.'

'I don't want people to know what I've got on the walls, whether I pray, or whether I'm married or divorced. It's disrespectful for you to write stuff like this. Do you understand?'

She nodded.

His expressionless gaze; he kept standing there for a bit. Then he left.

She immediately stuck the notebook in a drawer.

The train is still in the meadow, waiting for oncoming trains. The heat outside creeps into the car as its metal roof is warmed by the sun. Harriet sees the two birds, standing there perfectly motionless, remembering, and suddenly she hears the familiar click of a photograph being taken. She turns to look at her father, but can't see his face for the camera in the way. He's still aiming the lens at her, has her in his sights, maybe he's going to take another picture. She likes it when he takes pictures of her; it makes her feel good when he does. Harriet smiles at him, showing her teeth and making a peace sign with one hand.

'No,' he says. He lowers the camera. 'Why would you monkey around?'

He puts down the camera, placing it on the table between them, and gazes off. Harriet wants him to give her another chance, but the moment has passed. She feels sad again; her feelings gathering under her eyelids, anxiety hammering in her chest, she looks down at the table. She doesn't want to start crying, Dad doesn't like it. And then Dad takes another picture of her. He fiddles with the camera, adjusting the aperture somehow. She looks out of the window. One of the birds is flying low across the tall grass; the other stays behind, watching. It, too, leaves after a moment.

'Now!' Dad hisses.

Everything happens fast. He gets up and she's just as quick. They take a few steps into the aisle, and she sees the shape of the conductor in the next car, heading into theirs. They hurry to the lavatory and close the door behind them. Dad locks it. But Harriet unlocks it right away.

'What are you doing?' he whispers, his eyes round and worried.

'If he sees there's someone in here, he might wait outside until we come out,' she replies.

He considers this for a moment, then nods. He stands with his head bent towards the door and listens to the steps of the conductor passing by just outside.

'New passengers,' says the voice on the other side of the door. 'Any new passengers from Stockholm?'

They wait, and then Dad cautiously opens the door and peers out. They exit quickly, sit down, blending in with the paying passengers. He gives her a little nod and she nods back. And her pulse is high and she feels nauseated, wants to vomit because she's doing something that's against the rules. But something even stronger spreads out inside her, a warmth, a tiny fire in her chest when she looks at him and he looks at her and they exchange smiles.

They're jibing.

Chapter 2

Oskar

The platform is hot and festering. The train is late and there haven't been any updates from the loudspeakers. When a voice overhead finally advises that the train is entering the station, the travellers are suddenly in a rush — everyone but his wife. Unbothered, she stays where she is, searching for something in her pockets. Oskar watches as she shoves her hands into her tight jeans, searches the pockets of her jacket, and her handbag, and at last she finds what she was after. It was a lighter. The train is coming, but now she wants a smoke.

'Shouldn't we board?' Oskar asks.

'I'm just going to have a cigarette.' She cups her hand around the flame even though the air is still, pulls a deep drag into her lungs. He waits. The scrape of suitcases very close, and the rush of morning traffic on some distant highway. It's another hot day. It's seven-thirty in the morning, it's 17 September, and this summer is never-ending. The platform is soon deserted, but she's smoking as though she knows the train isn't going anywhere without her.

When they board, he walks close behind her, and he catches a faint whiff of the perfume she was wearing yesterday. She moves briskly through the narrow aisle, and he observes the gazes of those who catch sight of her for the first time. He always does that, even now he does it. She takes a seat by the window, just grabs a random spot. Oskar stays in the aisle, looking down at their tickets. 'These aren't our seats,' he says.

'It doesn't matter, you can see the train is empty,' she says.

No, it's not empty at all, and there will be more passengers boarding along the way. Oskar doesn't like sitting in other people's seats, because it means he can't relax. And if someone is suddenly standing over him, clearing their throat, pointing at their ticket, and Oskar has to grab all his things and trudge off, he'll feel degraded. He sits down across from her. The train leaves the platform without making any noise, glides over Central Bridge, the rails are slick and don't make a sound, the sea is calm on both sides; even the Baltic looks inviting today, just small ripples where the current is strong. The train slowly accelerates, and as it enters the tunnel through the bedrock, he catches sight of his reflection in the window and reacts, as always, with minor discomfort; he wants to look away quickly but something makes his gaze linger and observe himself in the dim yellow glow. Once, when he was a kid, he drew dicks on the wall of the school bathroom with a marker and a teacher caught him red-handed. They made him go to the school counsellor, who sat behind a large desk and fixed a stern gaze on him and said, 'Here's a funny thing. When I met all you new pupils on the first day of school, I noticed you in the crowd and knew right off the bat that something was up with you. I thought: This one is going to be a problem. I could see it in your face – I saw that your inner pressure was high.'

That phrase has stuck with him ever since, his inner pressure. He looks at himself in the window, his serious expression, his wide mouth, its lips that don't close all the way. His brown eyes, which look nearly black in the dim light. Is this a man with high inner pressure? He still doesn't know what that means.

A conductor welcomes them onboard over the loudspeakers. The man is a little too enamoured by his own voice, says more than is necessary, and Oskar has the urge to exchange a glance with her over it, because both of them find that type of person annoying. But of course this isn't the right time. Anyway, her eyes are already closed. He knows her, knows what she's doing; she doesn't want to sleep, she just doesn't want to talk.

She seldom does, these days. He thought about it yesterday, during the argument that began in the morning and then lasted through the evening and night, how wordless long stretches could be. A few sentences to ignite it all, her shouts and his, and they flung wild accusations, but mostly

15

they sat there in silence. As if they both realised there was no point in trying to solve this issue with words. At last she lit two candles there in the kitchen. It was so odd – as if she wanted to make things a little cosy as they fell apart. Maybe she thought it would be possible to live there, inside that silence. Have a sandwich, read a newspaper. And now, early in the morning, they were still silent. They closed the door to the apartment and walked without a word down to Central Station, and now that they're on the train they've slid even deeper into silence. If this is the end of their story, it's a quiet one. At the beginning of their relationship, they talked non-stop. Their first date at that bar. Or the train trip just before it, when they met for the first time. That legendary story! Tell the train story again! They've told it so many times, to one another and to other people; she once said she can hardly tell what's true any more. But he remembers every detail.

Years ago, he was sitting by himself on a train from Gothenburg to Stockholm. The train stopped at one station longer than normal. Eventually the passengers looked up curiously from their newspapers – what's going on? Why aren't we moving? No messages over the loudspeakers. Fifteen minutes passed, the mood growing increasingly anxious as the passengers found their afternoon plans sabotaged. Suddenly the door to his car slammed open and she thundered in, hurrying through the train. She was wearing a leather jacket over a long dress that had tiny white buttons down the front. She threw herself into a seat across from

Oskar. Only then did he notice that she had a gash on her head, and a trickle of blood right by her eyebrow. Then the two police officers appeared. They came from the same direction as she had and weren't in a rush. They knew she couldn't get away. They moved slowly through the car, their radios making noise, whistling and crackling, and now they had everyone's attention. They stopped by her seat. One of the officers was stockier than the other, with red, angry spots between his eyes and on his forehead. He looked inflamed. The policeman pointed at her. 'You,' he said. 'You're coming with us, off the train.'

'No,' she replied.

'Yes, you're getting off right now.'

'Why?' she asked.

'You know why,' the officer said.

'No I don't. I need to go to Stockholm, and I plan to get there on this train.'

The policeman took a step towards her, and she cried out, sudden and shrill: 'Do not touch me!'

The officer immediately backed off, as though he felt hurt because she'd managed to frighten him. 'Am I going to have to drag you out of here?' he said.

'But I told the conductor!' she said. 'I didn't have time to buy my ticket at the station, and when I was going to pay here on the train there was some issue with the machine. I can pay when we get to Stockholm.'

'That's not how it works,' said the officer.

'But I've got money on my card, this isn't my fault.'

'Listen here,' said the other officer, taking a step forward. 'You are delaying this whole train simply because you refuse to do as we say. You don't have a ticket, and you have to get off this train.'

She ignored them, opened a magazine, and Oskar noticed the officers exchanging terse nods, hardly visible to anyone else on the train, an agreement between them that had been refined by many years of handling crap in service on the streets. Then they grabbed her. He's not sure if they were too rough, but she screamed, and her cries got even louder as they managed to haul her into the aisle. She held onto a seat headrest, and now something happened in the car. The passengers, who had thus far sat quietly watching the scene, began to protest. Cries rang out from all directions.

'What are you doing?'

'Let her go!'

'She said she'd pay in Stockholm!'

She kept shouting that she wanted to pay her way, and the situation must have suddenly felt untenable to the officers, with all the passengers taking her side. The two of them didn't quite know what to do. Some passengers had stood up to see what was going on, and that was when Oskar made up his mind. He raised his voice. 'How much is the ticket?' he asked the officers. 'How much does she owe?'

'How should I know?' said one officer.

'Two hundred,' she said. 'It cost two hundred kronor.'

Oskar took out his wallet and removed two hundred-kronor bills, which he offered to the officers.

'I don't want it,' said the fat one. He chuckled nervously. 'I'm not the conductor.'

Oskar handed the money to her instead.

'There,' he said, turning to the officers. 'Now she has money for her ticket. Now you can go.'

The police officers were at a loss, as if the situation had become too much for them, too philosophical. The other passengers had begun to lend a hand: encouraging voices all through the compartment; the car wanted the police to leave. And so they did, to mild cheering, and she pressed her palms together and gestured at the passengers. 'Thank you,' she mimed, then sat back down and leaned towards Oskar, taking his hands. 'I'll pay you back as soon as we get to Stockholm,' she said. 'We'll go straight to an ATM.'

The train left the station and the Swedish summer passed by outside the window, and onboard the train all the passengers were transformed. They were no longer alone; they were united. They had stood up for this woman and they had done so together. Everything was easy and smooth, all down the rows of seats, gentle smiles in the car, for she was theirs now, they had kept her, a trophy of their goodness, gleaming there in seat 27.

Then the conductor came in, her black leather case with its brass details over her belly. She checked the tickets of new passengers and, when she got to Oskar's seat, the woman bolted to her feet. She crumpled the two bills she'd just been given and threw them at the conductor's chest. 'Here's your fucking money.'

A slight wave of unease in the car now. Because, was that really necessary?

The conductor bent down, picked up the bills, and smoothed them out. 'You didn't have a ticket,' she said calmly. 'So I offered you the chance to buy one onboard. To buy a ticket onboard the train, you must pay cash. You didn't have any cash. You wanted to pay with a card, but that's not possible. There's not even the technology to do that. So I told you, if you don't have a ticket or the money to pay for one, you must get off the train. Then you called me a whore.' She took out a ticket, made a careful note on the small piece of paper, and handed it to the woman. 'And you know something,' she continued. 'I don't like being called a whore.'

The conductor moved on. Uncertainty spread through the car. She'd called her a whore? Who was this woman everyone had stood up for? He hardly dared to look at her, glanced at her from the corner of his eye, the black hair she'd tucked behind her ears but which kept falling over her face. Oskar's father had once told him that as soon as he saw a beautiful woman he should imagine what she would look like skinned. That way, you don't run the risk of being blinded by anyone's beauty. The train sped up, they were late. When dusk began to fall they were still in central Sweden, and he saw the wires running alongside the track, dipping and rising, the electric fences gleaming in the setting sun, a bright yellow field, coming and going, and when it was fully dusk he saw her reflection, a double exposure in the window. Oskar gazed out at the small communities, and lights flickered and came on outside the houses. For a few moments they were racing an articulated lorry on one of the highways. Exploding past calm lakes where the Styrofoam buoys bobbed above fish traps, they travelled into the summer night and all the while he stole glances by way of her reflection in the window, couldn't stop looking at her.

When they arrived at the Central Station she said she thought there was an ATM on Vasagatan, and Oskar asked if they shouldn't grab a drink instead. In retrospect, he's never quite been able to explain it. She was much younger than him, and this wasn't in his nature: he'd always had a hard time approaching women, he tended to be shy and unable to speak. Sometimes he thinks about the person he was during that time. He used to visit crowded bars just before closing time, stand at the bar with a beer, and let the crowds decide where he should go. Why did he do that? Maybe to feel physically near to something; he was surrounded by bodies there. And if he spotted some woman he was interested in, he could let himself be carried in her direction, let himself be pressed to her side. In and out of various bars he went, always alone. And he often rounded off his evening at a nightclub, where he would seek out the gigantic speakers, stand by the subwoofer, which was taller than he was, and let the sound bore through his body. The music entered his bones, made his skeleton ache, and when he staggered to the street, into the night, he heard nothing, felt nothing, saw only the distorted faces of those he passed in the Stockholm night, with a feeling of relief; perhaps he had done away with himself.

That's why Oskar was so surprised at himself when he suggested they grab a drink. He didn't talk to women like that. But he knew from the start that she was different, and he'd felt a rising panic the closer they got to Stockholm. A fear that she would vanish and be gone for ever. He wanted her. He imagined her skinned, and he wanted her without skin too. They walked through Central Station and out onto Vasagatan. Stockholm was humid: wet streets, a rain shower must have come through, but it was still warm as they pulled their suitcases behind them. They went into a bar that was showing sports on muted screens, and sat down at a window table. He ordered two steaks, but she didn't touch her food. She drank beer and ate nuts; she would squirrel five or six in her palm and then portion them into her mouth one by one. She asked what he did for work and he said he was a real-estate agent, and she snickered and said, 'You don't look like one.'

'What do you do?' he asked.

'I'm a librarian.'

At that he let out a guffaw, loud and full of a confidence he didn't really possess. 'A librarian,' he said. 'You *really* don't look like a librarian.'

She shrugged.

'I love books,' she said.

'What's the most beautiful sentence you've ever read in a book?' he asked.

'Sometimes . . .' She paused to think, to make sure she got every word just right. 'Sometimes I can feel my bones straining under the weight of all of the lives I'm not living.'

'Wow,' he said. 'Sounds depressing.'

'Yeah,' she said with a laugh. 'I often feel down when I think about everything that never happens.'

She took out a cigarette. She would smoke them halfway and bend them into the ashtray as though she was suddenly tired of smoking and had decided to quit. And soon she would light another one. And when she said something important she placed a hand on his arm, as though this were perfectly natural. All the while he wanted to get closer to her; the edge of the table chafing his belly. She carefully cut the letter O from her steak, O as in Oskar, and took the letter of meat between her thumb and index finger and handed it to him. He didn't understand what it meant.

Around her wrist she wore a little wooden medallion, and it dangled onto the table as they talked so he caught it between thumb and index finger to take a closer look. On one side was her name, and on the other side it said 'Dad'.

'Nice,' he said.

'Oh,' she replied, as if she felt a little embarrassed.

'Do you have a good relationship with your dad?'

'I wouldn't say that. Our relationship has always been a little odd. He's pretty bad at showing emotion. He's never said he loves me, for instance.'

'Have you told him you love him?'

'Once, when I was little. Know what his response was? He didn't say anything, he just sat there.' She stared at the table, a tentative smile on her lips.

'What would happen if you called right now and told him you love him?' Oskar asked.

She laughed, shaking her head and looking out of the window. And he was starting to get tipsy, so he took out his phone. He had just been hired for his first job with a real-estate firm, and on his first day he was given his own cell phone; no one else he knew had one. He set the phone on the table in front of her. 'Call him now!' he said. 'Call him and tell him you love him.'

'He'll just think it's a joke,' she said.

'Call him!'

This was the first time he saw something different in her eyes. She had been so full of confidence. From that very first moment, even as the police tugged at her, it was like she knew no one could touch her. But now something happened; girlish features appeared on her face as she looked down at the table, and she turned around to get the bartender's attention, to order another drink.

'Call him right now!' he cried.

She couldn't say no. In hindsight, he knows why. She was used to being the one who came up with crazy ideas; this was just the sort of thing she might have suggested. She picked up the phone and started dialling, and Oskar moved to sit on her side of the table, their temples close and the phone between their ears. Her father picked up.

'Hi, Dad, it's me.'

'Hi, you.'

'Did I wake you up?'

'No, no,' he replied. 'Where are you?'

He remembers her father's gravelly voice, which had the tendency to crack now and then as though his vocal cords were damaged, and she explained that she was at a restaurant. 'So,' she said. 'I was just calling to say . . .' Oskar felt her body stiffen. 'I was just calling to say . . . that I love you.'

'Bitty,' her father responded, and he inhaled sharply.

'Bitty,' she repeated – and burst into tears. Oskar looked on, dumbfounded, as she sobbed, and after a moment she cleared her throat, getting control of herself. 'Well, talk soon,' she said, and she hung up and another wave of grief came over her, making her slim body shake slightly. She brought her hands to her eyes and he just sat there, nailed to his chair, unsure of how to comfort her. He was clueless, had no idea about what he would eventually learn and even become part of, be transformed by. He didn't understand that he had opened the door to something at the very core of her. She let out an audible breath, which echoed through the bar, as though she had grown weary of herself. She took out another cigarette then immediately changed her mind, put it back in the pack. Oskar brushed away the hair that had fallen into her face. He let his hand linger there, cupping her cheek, and they looked at one another and he remembers how difficult it was for him to look her in the eyes, he had to force his wavering gaze back again and again.

That's when they kissed for the first time. And he doesn't know how long the kiss lasted, he only remembers that when he looked up again they were all alone in the bar. The lights had come on, closing-time clatter, and staff were trying to clean them out of the place.

'Is the night over now?' she asked with a little laugh.

'I don't know,' he replied.

'We must have another drink in us,' she said.

And they went out into the warm night, Vasagatan crowded even though it was past midnight. They passed some closed pubs and Oskar recalls that she suggested they go to the skatepark at Humlegården where people hung out at night. She liked to sit there and watch the skaters fall, she said, because there was nothing she found more amusing than to see guys getting hurt. Sometimes he thinks about that night and wonders why he didn't see the red flags – or, that's not true: he saw them, but he was merely fascinated, interpreted them as something else. 'Tell me about your family,' he said, and she said she had a sister, but they weren't in touch at all. They hadn't seen each other since they were kids, she said. 'Why aren't you in touch?' he asked.

'Because she doesn't like me,' she replied.

What about her mother? No, she hadn't been in touch with her since she was a kid either. She didn't want to go into details, but her parents had divorced, which had resulted in a custody battle; the family was split up. She cracked the door into a family in ruins, and she was hardly moved when she talked about it. Just amusing random facts in the Stockholm night. He should have stayed away from her, there was so much that was broken. She rendered him totally speechless one time that night. They were walking right behind a man

26

around his own age who had some injury and was dragging one leg behind the other, and suddenly she started imitating his gait, limping the same way, just for a few seconds, and then she stopped. He didn't see the point, it was simply cruel. It made her seem immature and uninteresting, but a second later she might say something he knew would stick with him for ever. 'Just once in a lifetime,' she said, as they walked along in the dark. 'Only once will you catch sight of yourself, and that moment alone will be either the happiest or bitterest moment of your life.'

He asked her to repeat what she'd just said, so she did.

'Has it happened to you?' he asked then. 'Have you caught sight of yourself?'

'No,' she replied. 'I'm still looking.'

All the while, the feeling of being on the cusp of an adventure, with no idea how it would end. Or, *she* was on the cusp of an adventure, and there were indications that she might let him come along. When they crossed Kungsgatan they passed a group of conference-goers, loud and in the swing of things. She turned around to watch them stagger off. 'Come on!' she called to Oskar. 'Let's follow them, they can decide our night!' That's exactly the person she was; she put him and the world together. She ran to catch up with the group and joined up with them, and they walked into a bar and she introduced them to the drinking games of her youth, and the bartender reluctantly went along with her, pouring a viscous but clear liquor she set on fire. She slammed her fist on the bar and made a face, and there were silly conversations that followed, which Oskar was sometimes part of and sometimes left out of, and then he observed those who were observing her, the men, seeing in their eyes what they saw in her. He saw them making fools of themselves for her, and sometimes she cast him a quick glance, as if to say, *this night is ours, yours and mine, and this is just some minor distraction.* She made him believe that they were only playing with those men, but in reality she was playing with him as well.

'I'm the fuck of the century,' she suddenly said to the conference-goers.

This declaration changed the mood; the men fell silent. They must have been around fifty, maybe older, and she was much younger. She repeated it, leaving longer gaps between the words: 'I. Am. The fuck. Of. The century.' The entire situation seemed threatening to Oskar, as the men approached her from all directions, predators now. He got up and pulled her out of there, and when they reached the street he felt nothing but distress. Why had she done that? He wasn't enough for her – and he never has been.

Of course everything the two of them have been through in the past twenty-four hours, leading up to this train trip, is a direct result of this very fact. Her lie, which was revealed yesterday. He could have predicted it if only he'd been a little more attentive on that first night, for the betrayal was already there within her; she was carrying it even then.

The train has exited the tunnel – they're on the other side of the hill, leaving the capital city behind. The passengers have begun to settle into their seats. Someone has opened a packed lunch; another lurches through the tilting car, vanishes into the lavatory and closes the door with a surprisingly loud bang. Outside the window, the rows of high-rises going by and the highways looping over and under each other, then the signs of something else, green patches amid the concrete, small wooded areas and lakes as the train pushes its way out of the subway and into the late summer. And then the train inexplicably slows down and stops. They're parked with a view of a meadow. They managed to travel for fifteen minutes before the train acted up. It's almost fascinatingly useless. No messages from the crew, Oskar stares down at the tabletop, feeling his irritation rise. His inner pressure increases. At last, the conductor who's in love with his own voice informs them they're waiting for an oncoming train.

He watches her as she pretends to sleep. A drop of sweat trickles down between her breasts and he wonders, for a split second, where it went after that.

The end of the legendary story of how they ended up together. They took a shortcut across Kungsträdgården and walked along Skeppsbron, went by way of Slussen up to Stigberget where her apartment was. By the time they arrived, it was getting light out, and she giggled when she couldn't find the right key, unlocked the door with an unsteady hand.

'I have to ask,' he said as he waited for her to get the door open. 'Did you have money on your card?'

She glanced up at Oskar. 'No,' she said.

And they went inside.

There it is, in all its glory, the epic tale of how they met. They've always recounted it as an awfully romantic story. But now, after everything that happened last night, it strikes him: their story began exactly as it ended, with a lie.

Chapter 3

Yana

She moves away from the clamour of the platform, walk-ing onto the tongue of asphalt between the two tracks. At the far end is a bench, and she sits down on it. It's deserted here, aside from the two conscripts who stand directly in front of her, and she lets her gaze rest on them as they chat. Their packs are by their feet, green bags the size of human bodies. One of the guys runs his index finger under his upper lip and scoops out the packet of *snus* there, and he bends down and almost tenderly wipes the tobacco onto the asphalt, where it gleams in the sun, reminding her of the snails she always saw after summer rains as a kid.

Yana hears the tracks ring and sees the locomotive appear far off down the line. The young guys in uniform pick up their big bags and walk back to the throngs on the platform to find their car, but she remains seated. When the train gets closer, she spots the engineer staring straight ahead with a vacant expression, and just as the locomotive is about to pass she slowly raises her hand to him. A solemn gesture, as though he were expected, coming with precious cargo. Their gazes meet for an instant and the engineer raises his hand in return. She can't explain why she did it; maybe because the engineer is part of this story too, because he's the one driving the train and it's an important train.

Yana boards, takes a seat in one of the booths in the buffet car, and places the photo album on the table in front of her. Suddenly she sends a grateful thought to her father. The only useful thing he did for her in the past twenty years was die, because his death led her to the photo album she's placed on the table before her. It started with a phone call one afternoon a month ago, a nurse from a hospice south of the city informing her that her father was in care there. The nurse had discovered that Yana was listed as next of kin in his records, and if she wanted to see her father before he died, now was the time. She thanked the nurse for the information and hung up. She hadn't seen her father in ten years, and the only contact they had was over the phone, each time she had a birthday. He would always call to congratulate her, their exchanges of words taut as steel cables on a bridge. She'd had no interest in her father when he was alive, and she didn't intend to start caring when he was dying, either. But it was as though the phone conversation with the nurse slowly ate at her that afternoon. He had listed her as next of kin, and somehow she saw this as an act of tenderness on his part. Was this his way of reaching out? Was he telling her he wanted to reconcile?

She went to the kitchen, tucked two pieces of bread in the toaster, her usual snack between lunch and dinner, and a memory of a hotel breakfast in her childhood popped up: the family on vacation, she doesn't recall where, just that it was hot and you couldn't walk barefoot on the stone slabs by the pool. A large buffet of sandwich toppings under glass domes, irresistible luxury, and she went back a number of times. Mom was delighted, calling each time Yana came to the table that she should take more, have another plate! And so she did: sausages and cheeses and doughnuts and chocolate croissants. She took two pieces of toast and spread a thick layer of Nutella on them. When she brought her toast to the breakfast table, she walked by Dad, who looked up from his newspaper and said, 'You're not going to give up until you weigh a hundred kilos, huh?'

Sometimes, when Yana is eating something she knows she shouldn't eat, she thinks of Dad's comment that day, and she usually giggles at it, and mumbles to herself: 'You won't give up until you weigh a hundred kilos, huh?'

Now Dad was dying, and Yana stood in the kitchen eating her toast, and then she lay down on the sofa, felt her heart beating fast and hard in her chest. She fell asleep after a while and later, when she woke up, it was dark outside. She made a snap decision, got up and called the hospital and asked which unit Dad was in. But there was silence on the other end, and a gentle 'ahem', and a voice that said: 'I'm very sorry, but your father has just passed away.'

The next day, she went to the facility. She was led into a white room next to the chapel. There was a candle burning on a table, and there lay Dad, a dark figure in white sheets. Someone had buttoned his shirt up all the way, his skin was pulled tight at his throat and she wanted to undo the top button; what if he can't breathe? An expression on his face that reminded her of when he was alive, something grave, a wrinkle of concern between his eyebrows; he looked just like when he was making dinner in the kitchen, as he stood hunched over a recipe and didn't want to be bothered. Those evenings full of lengthy meal preparations. Mom and Dad opening a bottle of wine, taking out salami and cheese. Mom told Dad about things that had happened at work, while Dad *hmm*ed and nodded and seasoned a sauce. Yana liked those moments, felt that maybe her parents still loved each other, after all. But there was always something about Dad when he was in the room, irritation always waiting in the wings. Mom placed a small bowl of cheese puffs in front of Yana, there in the kitchen; Dad noticed the bowl but said nothing, reluctantly let it pass. But the room grew smaller.

Dad, always tense and closed off, and even if he didn't say a word the whole family was governed by his mood. When Mom wasn't home, he spent a lot of time trying to find her. He would call her over and over, and wouldn't stop until she came home. All the strange things Yana saw him do when he thought he was alone. A number of times she had seen Dad stand all alone in the kitchen early in the evening. He had bought steak at the market hall; he slowly unfolded the snow-white paper and drove his fist into the meat. And again. Hard, heavy blows right into the raw steak.

Once, when the whole family was walking around town, a man happened to bump into Dad with his shoulder. Dad turned around and asked what his problem was, and the man replied: 'Watch where you're going.' Dad took a step towards the man and the man did the same. Dad, his eyes crazy, had his phone in hand and flung it full-force into the street. The phone shattered into a thousand pieces. The man was astonished as he looked down at the destruction Dad had wrought upon his own property. He backed off and vanished. He had discovered it too: Dad was a loose cannon and you'd better watch out.

Yana said nothing, there at Dad's deathbed; she did nothing, just stood there for a moment and looked at him. He looked exactly the way she remembered, only thinner. It was clear he had been sick for a long time. She looked at his skinny arms, visible beneath his sleeves, looked at his gnarled hands and a watch that had become too large and was hanging loose around his wrist.

He didn't give up until he weighed forty kilos.

Yana went home, and the most unexpected thing happened after Dad's death; she started to think about Mom again. Yana hadn't spared her a thought for years. Ever since her mother had vanished twenty years ago, Yana had been determined to erase her from her life. She doesn't exist, she never existed in the first place. But now Mom was appearing again, showing up in new memories that wouldn't leave Yana alone. A morning when the sun is blazing beyond the blinds, Yana stays in bed with Mom. She's hot, her forehead shiny, her hair everywhere, clinging to her temples. They're on their backs, Mom's round breasts have spread out across her ribcage, the soles of their feet pressed together, they're cycling in the air, looking up at the ceiling and whispering to each other in the dawn light. Sudden memories of Mom's laugh, like she was clearing her throat but lost control; Mom's lovely line of teeth when she smiled, the scents of her – perfume and sweat and something else, something strange and dangerous, adrenaline?

A memory of standing in the doorway to their bedroom after a nightmare. Afraid to approach, Yana just stood there crying silent tears and Mom woke up and said, 'Oh, sweetie,' in the dark and patted the sheets gently a few times. 'Come here, sweetie,' and Yana crept under the blanket and Mom held her and said, 'I'll take care of you, I'll always take care of you.' She whispered it so many times it sounded like a little song, a melody someone was playing, again and again, until she fell asleep. In the car, when they had to go somewhere and had been sitting in silence for a while, Mom would place the hand that had just been on the stick shift on Yana's knee and say, 'It's you and me, sweetheart.' And that was all, the journey continued.

Yana took care of her father's funeral. She made the neces- sary calls, to the tax authority, the landlord, and the electric company; she booked a meeting with the funeral home. She sat indoors for days, planning psalms for the service, compos- ing the obituary for the morning paper, and all the while she pictured Mom. When the day of the funeral arrived she put

36

on a new black dress and just as she was about to leave she collapsed on the floor in the front hall. She couldn't breathe. She called 112, could hardly produce a word; she said: 'I think I'm dying.' She lay there waiting for help to arrive, and after a few minutes she heard the ambulance sirens on the street outside and two paramedics were soon at her side, examining her. They said it wasn't necessary for her to go to the hospital. Instead they suggested she go to the urgent mental health clinic. She could ride in the ambulance, they said. She met with a psychiatrist. He was young and had a gentle smile. He asked her to tell him why she was there, but she couldn't answer. He said that what she had experienced was a panic attack. It feels like you're going to die, but you aren't.

'What do I do to keep it from happening again?' Yana asked.

'Treatment is evolving,' he replied. 'It used to be that a doctor would always ask, "What's wrong with you?" Now, we're much more interested in knowing: "What happened?"'

She liked this, because it was such a forgiving question. And then she told him, from the beginning, about a mother who disappeared one day when Yana was a little girl, and a father who stopped being a father, and all the years that passed during which she didn't think about Mom at all, and then Dad's death the other day and what it set in motion inside her. When she was finished, she was struck by the realisation that this was the first time she'd ever told anyone what had happened to her. 'It feels good to talk about it,' she told him.

'That's great,' he replied. 'No one can bear this sort of thing all on their own. If you can, share it with more people.'

She was given a prescription for antidepressants, went home and called in sick for a few days. The doctor said the medication would calm her heart, but it wasn't true. It continued to pound wildly, and the memories of Mom kept coming. She spent two weeks in bed, image after image from her childhood revealing itself, and the psychiatrist's words flowed through her, his question that she'd slowly taken on as her own.

What happened?

Yesterday afternoon she went to Dad's apartment, the very apartment she grew up in and hadn't been in since she moved out at eighteen. The apartment was being readied for new tenants, and this was her last chance to take anything before the place was emptied and cleaned out. Someone unlocked the door for her and vanished, calling from the stairwell on their way down: 'Just close the door behind you when you're done.' And she stood there in the hall for a moment, then took a few steps and peered into her childhood bedroom. Dad had turned it into an office. A computer stood on a desk. All her things were gone, traces erased. But the sun fell through the tall window today just as it had back then. She sat down at the desk. Beside it was a bookcase full of binders, their spines carefully labelled. She saw her name on one binder. It contained copies of cell phone bills. She ran her hand gently over the yellowed documents. So Dad had saved them. He had kept them for all these years. This had been one of their last silent fights, maybe *the* last one? She moved out just a few months later.

She had been in high school, close to graduating. Her birthday was early in the year, so she was one of the first in her class who could sign up for their own phone plan at eighteen. Having your own plan was a status symbol, and two classmates who were otherwise uninterested in her came up to her one break and wanted to check out her phone. Another couple of girls joined in, and there she stood, in the centre of it all. They asked Yana if she could help them get phone plans. During lunch, they went to the shopping centre. She got to be the leader, and she did all the talking in the store while the others stood a few steps behind her. They had some special offer, a free phone if you signed a one-year contract, and she helped them all, phones and envelopes with SIM cards were passed around to each and every one. And the news spread; more people approached her the next day. She was important, she was sitting on the golden tickets to her classmates' adult lives, and she enjoyed passing them out. It went on like that for a few weeks that winter. After a while the first phone bills showed up, one after the next, each time she came home from school there were new envelopes on the floor of the front hall. She administrated them out to her classmates, and after a few weeks the reminders showed up, with a sterner tone: the bills must be paid immediately or they would be sent to the debt collectors. She begged her classmates to pay up, and they promised they would: they accepted the reminder notices, stuffed them in their backpacks. Not a single one of them paid. One day, when she got home from school, Dad was already there. He called to her from the kitchen. He was holding some envelopes from a collections agency and asked her what was going on, and, crying, she had to confess what she'd done. Dad spoke softly, rapidly, wanted information. How many contracts had she signed in her name? At which store? Then he closed the door to his office. They never spoke of it again. That's how she remembers her childhood with him, like a long silence between them. Yana had been eleven when Mom disappeared. Those first years without her, when she walked around the apartment in that peculiar void. When she and Dad ate breakfast together on weekday mornings he sometimes didn't say a single word to her. They had a dog called Loser. He was her only company during those years. She gingerly paged back through the phone bills, saw Dad's handwriting in ink, on the top of each page: '*Outstanding debt.*' To think he kept the bills for all these years, patiently waiting for the debt to be paid.

She got up and went to the hall that led to her parents' bedroom. The bed was unmade, the blankets in the shape of an S, as though he'd left one last signature. The long row of wardrobes along one wall. Dad's jackets were still hanging there, and shoes that hadn't been used in a long time were covered in a thin layer of dust. The clothes were gone from Mom's wardrobes, there was a vacuum cleaner there now, other cleaning supplies, and at the back of it Yana found a brown moving box with Mom's name on it. She picked up the box, which was heavier than she'd expected, and placed it on the bed. Inside was an old camera bag and some lenses, carefully wound in bubble wrap and rubber bands. She picked one of them up and weighed it in her hand, grabbed another one. She lined them up on the bed. They were ancient, and Yana didn't understand. Mom hadn't even owned a camera, had she? There was also a collar in there, one that looked like it had belonged to an animal, with a wooden bangle; on one side was Mom's name, and on the other it said 'Dad'. At the bottom of the box were nine photo albums. Eight of them were full of pictures of eagles, each one grainy, taken from a distance. In the ninth, which had a purple pleather cover and was at the very bottom, she found something entirely different, and those photos brought her here to this train.

This is one of the new high-speed trains; it tilts to be able to maintain maximum speed through the curves, and she has to hold her coffee cup down on the table as the train bends towards a small lake. She places a hand on the photo album, lets it linger there. Ever since she saw those pictures last night, she's been trying to recreate that day from twenty years ago, the last time she saw her mother. Mom and Dad fought all day long. It never stopped. At her bedtime that night, they were still shouting at each other. Yana, who always tried to eavesdrop on her parents, didn't want to hear this time. They were saying unforgiveable things. The argument moved through the apartment and she was relieved when they ended up in the bathroom, because from there their voices sounded dull and strange, as though they were shouting into pillows. At last everything was quiet, and then came the familiar sounds of Mom getting ready for bed: her strong stream of urine on the porcelain of the toilet, the tap in the bathroom running

41

for too long, because she wanted the water to be cold. Dad was still up and she listened to his steps; he never settled down that night, kept walking around, standing up, sitting down.

When Yana woke up the next day, both of them were gone. She found only a note on the kitchen table, signed 'Mom & Dad', but in Dad's handwriting. They would be gone all day and would return home that evening, but there was food in the fridge. And 'don't forget to feed Loser'. Yana waited for her parents. The day was long and hot. They lived on the top floor of an old building with a metal roof, and she opened the windows and the city noise filled the apartment. She knew, could sense, that something wasn't right. She called Dad's cell phone many times, but he didn't pick up. When she called Mom, a phone on the kitchen table vibrated: of course, she had forgotten it, left it at home. She waited anxiously, constantly moving from room to room, Loser following her, settling in her lap. And late that night she finally heard noise from the elevator, the unique sound signature that belonged to Dad, his dragging steps. And he came in, kissed her on the forehead, and said that Mom wasn't coming back. He went to his room. Dad had hung his jacket from a chair, and something white was sticking out of its pocket. Two train tickets. Destination: Malma Station.

She recalls thinking it sounded so beautiful. She could picture the station and she liked to fantasise about it, and no matter the time of year it was always summer at Malma Station. Mighty winds rustled the great treetops above the platform. Malma expanded within her and grew larger. She read about the tiny community online, looked at it from above on Google Maps. A small village concentrated around a train station and a main street. A grocery store, a bakery café, a shoe shop and a few houses, maybe fifteen of them, all in a row along the street. And around the village, miles and miles of forest.

The restaurant car is still empty. She removes the lid of her coffee cup, letting it cool. She opens the photo album, and on the first page is a caption, written in pen by a child: 'Bitty's funeral, August 1976.' And beneath that, her mother's name: 'HARRIET.'

The first photo shows a girl of around eight. Yana can tell it's her mother. Tangled black hair; no one has run a brush through it in a long time. Dressed all in black from head to toe. She's sitting on a train, gazing dreamily out of the window. A camera bag by her side. The next picture was taken around the same time, the very same scene, just seconds later. But this time the girl is closed off, looking down at the table in front of her. It looks like she's near tears. Yana turns the page and there's another picture, taken somewhere else. Her mother as a little girl, at a train station. She's sitting on a bench with her hands covering her face. Above her is a sign with the station name, and it says 'Malma Station'.

Last night she sat on the edge of her dead father's bed, the photo album in her lap, and realised: there have been multiple trips to Malma Station.

The first one took place in the seventies. Mom was a little

girl at the time, she and her father took the train to Malma Station, to bury someone named Bitty – a pet of some sort? The second trip was on 17 September 2001. Mom is now an adult and deeply unhappy in her relationship with Dad. In the midst of their worst crisis, as their relationship is crumbling, they suddenly decide to leave their daughter home alone and board a train to Malma Station. Mom never returns from that journey.

What happened?

This is the third trip. Yana is tracing the events of the two previous trips, looking for the shape of a story that spans decades. She pages through the photographs in the album, and they blend with the images of Mom she carries inside her, the brief memories that won't give her any peace, and Sweden passes outside the train window. She gazes out at the sodden autumn meadows, feels a chill in her chest but a warmth in her belly, and she suddenly gasps for air and listens for her pulse as it throbs through her body. Her heart is skipping every third beat. It feels like you're going to die, but you aren't.

Chapter 4

Oskar

What is he doing here? Why did he even agree to come on this trip? As though they didn't have more important things to deal with. Why aren't they at home with Yana, who must be worried? Where are they going? All Oskar knows is their destination: Malma Station. What will happen there, he doesn't know. Harriet has asked him to be patient, says it will be clear when they get there. He looks around the train car, the scene almost looks comical with the open newspapers everywhere. Everyone's reading about the collapsed Twin Towers, every last passenger. It's been a week since the attack, but the media aren't about to stop covering it. He can't read about it, he reacts the way he always does when it feels like the world is falling apart – he shuts down.

He looks at Harriet. She appears to have fallen asleep for real. It's so strange that she can sleep through this. It was the same thing yesterday: in the midst of all the insanity she got tired and went off to brush her teeth. Then she lay down and was out like a light. He couldn't relax; he lay awake for a long time, thinking of all the things they'd said to each other that day. Had he gone too far? He must have. He had grabbed her too roughly, and he could tell at once it was wrong, that he'd crossed a line. But the things she was saying were so cruel and surreal. Some of the accusations were new to him. She said she wished they'd never met and that it had been a mistake to move in together, but, above all, that it had happened against her will. She hadn't wanted that, she said. They'd never agreed to live together. 'You forced your way in!' she shouted. 'You just showed up with your fucking suitcases and forced your way in! You never asked. I never wanted you to move in!' He was at a total loss, and Harriet fell silent because it was like she knew she had fired a weapon that had never been used before. Because if what she said was true, their entire relationship was based on a violation. Had she said it to hurt him? Or was it genuinely the way she remembered it? It had always been like this between them: they would experience something together and later on she would recast it in her mind, the incident now so twisted and warped that he could no longer recognise it.

Oskar recalls back in the beginning, just a few days after the legendary train trip where they met. They were taking a walk in the Söder neighbourhood of the city, the low autumn sun shining straight into their eyes on Hornsgatan. Harriet told him that this was her childhood neighbourhood and reeled off a bunch of facts that were interesting only to her – that shoe store, it used to be a tobacconist. They walked by her old school, gazed at the schoolyard and its netless basketball hoops, the white shapes on the asphalt for ball games whose rules were long forgotten. A breeze blew over them, the sound of dry leaves scraping across the schoolyard. She showed Oskar the narrow alleyway where her father had once taught her to roller-skate. Dad had removed the toe stops from the skates, because he said they were for wimps, and when he tied her laces she was so scared she almost burst into tears, because how was she supposed to brake? She asked her dad to hold her hand, and he promised he would, but he let go, after all – how else was she supposed to learn? She kept going faster and faster down the gentle slope, and she fell right here. Harriet pointed to a spot on the pavement where she had lain, where the blood from her knees had trickled onto the ground. She walked on, and as she passed that spot she avoided it so as not to step on herself lying there.

On a street just behind Mariatorget, she pointed up at an old, rusty-red façade. 'That's where I lived.'

It wasn't much to look at, a row of windows on the fourth floor, but she stood there in silence for a moment, gazing up at them. 'Should we go up and ring the bell?' she asked.

'You can't do that,' he replied.

'Sure you can.'

'But wouldn't you have to call first, and ask if you can come?'

Harriet said, 'Stop,' and tugged his arm to lead him to the front door. When a man with a cane came out they slipped in and, as they stood facing each other in the pale light of the elevator, he recalls that she giggled and took his hand. They rang the doorbell and a dog howled and a muted voice told the animal to calm down. It was an older woman who opened the door, the little dog stiff with fear in her arms. Harriet explained that she had lived there as a child and asked if it would be possible to have a look around, and the old woman smiled. 'Haven't I seen you before?' she asked.

'Have you?'

'I think so – haven't you stood on the street looking up here now and then?'

'Yes,' Harriet said. 'Maybe I have.'

'You're welcome to come inside,' said the woman.

Harriet set her purse down in the front hall and took a few steps into the apartment, walking around the way you do when you've just checked into a hotel, as though they would be staying here for a while. She went to one of the bedroom doors and peeked in. 'This was Dad's room,' she said, running her hand down the doorframe, feeling the handle. 'When I was little, we didn't have any doors in the apartment. It was some idea of Dad's, that we shouldn't have secrets from each other. None of the rooms had a door.' She laughed, gazing back out to the hall. 'Not even the bathroom; there was only a curtain.'

She went into the kitchen, opened one of the drawers and had a look; it made Oskar a little nervous, it was like she kept overstepping the woman's hospitality. There was another bedroom in the apartment, and that had been her room when she was little. She took a step inside it and tried to orientate herself. 'There were two beds here,' she said. 'I slept there,' she continued, pointing to one corner. 'And my sister was across from me.' She caught sight of something on the floor by one wall, and kneeled. She bent towards it. 'Oh my God,' she said. 'Feel this.'

He ran his fingertips along the skirting board; the wood was scratched, and although it had been painted over with white paint he could feel that the skirting board was worn down. 'What is it?' he asked.

'My rabbit,' she said.

This was the first time Oskar had heard about the rabbit her father had given her when she was little. Its cage had stood in the corner and it had scraped the wall with its claws, through the wire.

'I had a classmate named Esther,' she said. 'She was popular, everyone wanted to be her friend. When she found out I had a rabbit, she asked if she could come over after school. The first thing she did was take him out of the cage. She cupped her hands around him and started to shake him, the way you do when you play Yahtzee. Then she set the rabbit down on the kitchen table and he was so shaken and dizzy that he started stamping one foot on the table. Esther yelled, "Look, he's dancing, he's dancing!" I wanted to pick him up and hold him, but I was too afraid to say anything. Esther picked the rabbit up again and started all over. "He's dancing! He's dancing!"'

The older woman didn't know what to say, and Oskar

didn't quite know either, because it seemed like Harriet was mostly telling this story to herself. Then she went back to the hall and out to the dining room, where she sat down in a chair, and it was some time before she asked the woman, 'May I sit here for a while?' And there she sat, perfectly still and gazing out of a window. Her forehead was sweaty; she cleared her throat oddly a few times. 'It's heavy, being here,' Harriet said. 'I can't get anywhere.'

'Yes, it must be strange . . . ' the woman tried, but fell silent.

They thanked the woman and left, heading back to Slussen, and he held her but didn't know what to say, because there was no way he could comprehend what he'd witnessed. They passed Medborgarplatsen and she suddenly wanted to go to a movie. *West Side Story* was playing. She had seen the movie before, and it was like she wanted to show it to him; as the film began she kept glancing at him to see how he reacted. But then she became absorbed in the story. Her face was blue, and he saw the tears running down her neck. She cried so hard she was shaking, but not at the part where everyone else cries, at the end, when Tony dies; she cried at the beginning, when they fall in love on the balcony. It was sweet: Harriet didn't cry for sorrow, she cried for love.

As they left, she spoke rapid-fire about the film, kicking pebbles ahead of her, and in that moment he felt that he'd never met someone so intense, so in the moment all the time, and yet so far away. Always present somewhere else, in something that had happened a long time ago, bent with her heart in her throat over bloodstains on the ground in Södermalm, or the rabbit scratches on the walls of her childhood, occupied with it, and then full-speed ahead into a different fairytale world, on the silver screen, engulfed in it, in tears. He walked right by her side after the movie, but she wasn't there, she wasn't with him; it was like he could never quite get a grasp on Harriet because she was always looking in a different direction. She asked to borrow his jacket, and he could tell she wasn't feeling well. He felt her forehead and said, 'You're burning up.' They decided to go home. And dusk fell quickly, condensation visible in the glow of the streetlights, which came on as they walked, the sky still pale blue but the moon out too. And he could see the first few stars, and the wind blew in from the sea and it was cold and inhospitable. They walked hand in hand.

Oskar dropped her off at home and said he would go to buy her some painkillers, and milk and honey; he would take care of her so she got well.

'I don't want you to leave me,' Harriet said.

'But I'll be right back,' he replied.

'Yeah, but still.'

He tucked her into bed with her clothes on before he left, and two hours later he rang her doorbell. When she opened the door, there he stood with three suitcases. She didn't say anything for a moment, and then she started to laugh.

'Are you moving in?' she asked.

'I thought I might,' he said.

They hauled the suitcases inside together, and Harriet couldn't stop laughing, because this was something she might have done.

She had a small balcony, and they took some tea and sat out there under blankets. A sliver of the sea was visible between two buildings; the water was black and glittered only when the Djurgården ferries passed by. She lit a candle, which kept going out in the cold breeze. It was late, and the buildings around them were dark, and they sat in that dim little box, chatting quietly.

Harriet was calm now; only her cigarette was anxious, a glowing dot moving in the darkness. She told him about a memory from when she was little and got stuck inside it, and eventually he interrupted her, asked how come she so often ended up there, in episodes from her childhood.

And that's when she told him that when she was a child, her mother had taught her that she must never regret something she'd already done. It was a mantra of hers, and suddenly she imitated her mother, a shrill complaint that echoed off the façades: 'What's done is done – no use dwelling on it,' she cried. You had to look forward, her mother claimed, because the future is unwritten and beautiful, full of possibility. But her mother was wrong, Harriet had come to realise – these days, she's pretty sure it's the other way around. Each time she thought about things that had happened to her, she thought of them in a new way. The stories kept changing. Maybe that was why she had become so obsessed with her childhood, because it was a living place where things seemed to move around. And her mother had been wrong about the future too. Increasingly, Harriet felt like there was no way she could change the path she had been set upon. She was a prisoner in the choices other people had made before her, was nothing but a bearer of the poison for the next generation.

'So everything that happens is predetermined?' he asked.

'That's right.'

'Then what's going to happen with you and me?' he asked.

'I'm afraid we're fucked.'

Oskar laughed. 'I don't want us to be fucked,' he said.

Harriet held the teacup, bent over it, letting the steam warm her cheeks. 'Maybe that's why we met. So that you could come and get me unstuck?'

They felt the first drops of rain. They looked up, she reached a hand into the air. She tucked the blanket tighter around her legs and everything was quiet, the courtyard below deserted. They looked at one another, and neither of them averted their eyes. After a moment, she giggled, a little embarrassed, and looked down and then up again, at him. It was just him and her and their eyes reaching deep, deep down.

'Finally,' he said. 'Now I've got you.'

'What do you mean?' she asked.

'Now you're here.'

They kissed, and down in the courtyard someone threw open a door and an old man came out with a bag of trash. He looked up at them and Oskar was struck by the notion that the man was clueless, he was only passing by, he had no idea about all the crucial moments that were happening here.

'Is it you and me now?' Oskar asked.

'Yes,' Harriet replied. 'Now it's you and me.'

He doesn't recall any euphoria or joy in that time on the balcony; he doesn't even remember feeling infatuated; all he remembers is a diffuse sense of melancholy. There was a sorrow within him now, the kind you feel when you've come into possession of something too valuable to lose.

'Tell me something about your childhood,' Harriet said.

'I hardly remember anything.'

'You remember something. Anything, whatever comes to mind first.'

'I remember the in-home daycare I went to when I was really small. Ulla and her husband Dag. Sometimes we'd go shopping, Dag would drive. I remember his brown leather gloves on the wheel. He liked to tease me and say he'd gotten us lost. He would be right outside the store, moaning and saying he had no idea where the store could be and I would point, laugh and point and tug at him: 'It's right there! It's right there!'

Harriet made a small sound and smiled. 'Another one,' she said.

'Another one ...' Oskar muttered. He nabbed her cigarette and took a drag, blew the smoke out into the night. 'I remember one hot summer day. I was six or seven. Mom was at work, and I lay in the sun all day, getting sunburnt all over my body on purpose.'

'Why?'

'Because I wanted Mom to rub lotion on me when she got home. If I got a sunburn, I knew I would get to feel her touch.'

'Oh, honey,' was all she said. Silence. She put a hand on his shoulder and he smiled at her – and all of a sudden he burst into tears. Out of nowhere. He's not a crier, he didn't even know if he'd ever cried as an adult. And he didn't know why he was sobbing now, but it was like she knew precisely. Harriet held him and comforted him and whispered to him that it feels good to cry, that you have to let it out sometimes. 'I'll take care of you,' she whispered. 'I'll always take care of you.' And he cried, unable to stop. And he didn't dare ask her, didn't dare to ask why he was so sad.

The train has not yet moved, a voice on the loudspeaker apologises for the delay, they're still waiting for an oncoming train.

Inside the car, through the open windows, the faint sounds of a summer that has hung on into September: a tractor ploughing a field in the distance. The wind catching hold of heavy treetops. A bumblebee slips into the compartment through one of the windows, sparking anxiety as it flies through the car. The passengers' eyes follow it, someone rolls up a newspaper. It's close to death, but it doesn't know that, and it gets lucky, happens to vanish out of a different window, it's captured by the wind and is gone. They're waiting for an oncoming train and all around is a silent irritation as the wait grows long, time leaking from the train straight down to the tracks. He brushes her foot and is afraid he's accidentally woken her. As though she deserved such consideration. It's mind-blowing that she can sleep through this.

At last the oncoming train arrives, passing at only a few

inches' distance outside like an instant solar eclipse. The car sways and then the train slowly starts moving again, gliding silently out of its hiding spot.

The shock awakens her, and she looks around. She orientates herself, and then their eyes meet. He wants to hate her, but maybe he can't. She's the girl who got her toe stops taken off, and ever since she's been unable to hit the brakes. How could any of this truly be her fault?

They look at each other and there is nothing else, only her dark brown gaze. Harriet smiles at him.

He thinks: Now I've got you.

She closes her eyes, and after a moment she's sleeping again.

Chapter 5

Harriet

Harriet tries to write her name on the dirty window with her index finger, but nothing happens and she realises the filth is on the outside. She looks through the layer of grime and sees the landscape rising and sinking, and there's only the occasional cloud in the sky, high and white like in a fairytale. She wants to paint a picture of the meadows, but her markers are in her backpack, which Dad has stowed up on the hat rack, and she doesn't dare ask him to get it down. She follows an electric wire with her eyes, watches it move in waves across the fields. Between two poles the cable makes a smile, and then there's another smile, and another. Those thin black lips, it's a mean smile. She's nestled deep into the hot seat and there's something about the sound of the train, the clatter of the rails and the wind through the open windows that makes it hard to keep her eyes open. She knows she must not fall asleep because, if she does, Dad might disappear.

Her eyes sting and she blinks so hard that everything goes black with tiny glowing spots flashing in the darkness like sparklers, and she opens her eyes again. Dad is right across from her. The electric wires sneer and the clouds curl and the wind whistles mournfully through the open windows, and maybe she could close her eyes just for a little bit, just for a few seconds. She lowers her lids and knows that what she's doing is dangerous, she has to open them soon, but the train is rocking her and the seat is warming her back, as though someone were holding her, and she falls asleep and dreams that she's on a train and someone warns of rain and shouts at her to close the window. It's Dad. She can't get the window closed, Dad is annoyed and has to show her how it's done, and it was so simple, Dad just sweeps his hand lightly and the window is closed and the rain roars on the roof of the train. She wakes up, orientates herself; where is Dad? He's still there. He's gazing out at the meadows, lifting his chin as though he sees something exciting, but loses interest again. Harriet wonders if she should say something to him, maybe ask him something about photography, because that often makes him want to talk. But she can't think of what to say.

She must not fall asleep again.

That car trip, she remembers so many details from it, even the ones that didn't mean anything. Alone with Dad in the Volvo, the one whose indicators flashed double time, which meant the car always seemed hysterical when it made a turn. He let her sit in front that time, the seatbelt slicing across her throat. Each time Dad lights a cigarette the car swerves, but otherwise his driving is calm and controlled. He always knows where he's going and is never surprised by anything. He's in no hurry when he shifts gears, unlike other drivers she's seen. He lets the engine relax completely before slotting the gear stick into its new position, and then he accelerates again. She travelled through patterns no one but her could see. The white stripes in different spots on the road, short and irritable on the sides, long and lazy in the middle. A secret game only she knew about: she would bite her tongue between every reflective post they passed. And the game became a compulsion, something she couldn't stop doing even though she wanted to. She thought up a new game. She labelled each oncoming car as either mean or stupid. It was immediately clear which car was which, based on their lights, and she sorted them in her mind with each passing one. Mean. Stupid. Stupid. Mean.

'What are you saying?' Dad asked.

'Nothing,' she was quick to respond.

'I can't concentrate when you're mumbling like that.'

Eventually they turned onto a highway, with signs for places that were hundreds of kilometres away, inconceivably far off. Always a wave of apprehension when she saw the 'beware wild animals' sign, because now the animals could simply bolt right out in front of the car, and they would crash and die, but Dad wasn't concerned, he didn't even slow down. Could it be that he hadn't seen the sign? She would watch out on his behalf, keep an eye on the side of the road. Dad listened to the radio, just the news. He reached out a finger of warning whenever something important came on and he wanted her to be quiet; again and again a finger in the air, even though she wasn't saying a word. This would be a long drive, Dad had said, and it was evening, she could see the sun flickering low between the tree trunks, and then it was just gone. The headlights clung to the forest, the signs started to shine back at them as they went, and she knew her task of watching out for wild animals was an important one, but at last she couldn't keep her eyes open and fell asleep.

When she woke up, she was in another world.

It was dark and she was cold. The car was parked, and her father was no longer at the wheel. The fog on the windows made it impossible to see out, and when she ran her hand over the window all she could see out there was darkness, and a few vague bright spots further off. She could hear her heart beating. She opened the car door, heard the fury of the highway very close by. The ground was wet, had it rained? She realised she was in a parking lot. She saw the glowing lights in the distance and began to run towards them, and now she could see that it was a gas station, a large canopy atop four white pillars, and a sign stretching into the sky, the price of gasoline at the top so the people on the highway could see it. The line of pumps making a dull rumble, sounding like threatened animals. She ran to the store, the door was closed and she cupped her hands over the glass and saw that it was dark inside. She did an about-face, looked around. Where was Dad? The traffic was louder now, and the neon was too bright and burned her eyes. And she ran off, spotted another building nearby, ran for its lights. It was a roadside pub and the door was heavy, the nearest patrons looked up as she came in, waited for the door to close again. She couldn't see her father anywhere, just strangers bent over their trays, eating. She hurried through the place, passed a fat woman at the cash register, rushed on, and there, in the corner by a window, illuminated by the yellow glow of the highway, was Dad. He looked up from his plate and caught sight of her, the fork in his hand froze mid-bite. Harriet took a few steps and stopped by his table.

'Oh, sweetie,' Dad said. 'You're up?'

She nodded and dug her fingernails into her thigh to keep from crying.

'Are you upset?' he asked.

She shook her head.

'Come here,' he said. Harriet went to him and he took her in as she stood there concentrating. He placed a hand on her head, let it fall back behind her neck. 'You were asleep, and I didn't want to wake you,' he said.

She nodded. And she knew she must not cry right now, because if she did he would have to be ashamed of her. She blinked hard and looked down at the floor, saw Dad's boots with their laces up to his shins. Dad stood up. 'Come on, let's get back on the road.' She followed him out, remembers his slow footsteps in the dark on the way to the car.

They got back on the highway and it had started raining, the windscreen wipers sweeping right to left, moving faster now. They didn't say anything more about what had happened, but she noticed something had changed, he let her play whatever she wanted on the radio. Most of the time he would turn down the volume when a song came on, but this time he let the music play. He asked if she missed her sister, and she said she did. Mom and Dad had been separated for three months, and this was the first time she would get to see her mother and sister again, and Harriet had lain awake at night, when she was supposed to be sleeping, trying to think of what her big sister looked like, but she failed to find her anywhere in her memory. She couldn't quite grasp her features. Mom and Dad always liked to say she looked like the opposite of Harriet. Harriet's dark hair, Amelia's blonde hair. Harriet's narrow nose, Amelia's wide one. 'You're each other's opposites!' Mom liked to say. She often said it with a laugh, shaking her head in some resigned sort of way, wondering how it could have turned out so screwy. But each time Mom said this, Harriet felt uneasy. She wanted to look like her sister, she wanted them to belong together. As far back as she could remember, she had tried to change herself so that her sister would like her, but all the while it was as if Mom sabotaged her attempts.

'You're like night and day!'

Harriet was always the one they thought was pretty, the one they called 'Princess' sometimes, the tall one: 'If you keep growing at this rate you could become a model when you're older, as long as you don't get your period too soon, because when you get your period you stop growing.' Amelia was the sister who could really become something. The one who could put two and two together. When Amelia lay on her bed in their room, studying for a test, her parents might tiptoe up and stand just outside to admire her. One evening Harriet heard her parents in the kitchen, fantasising about all the things her older sister could become. She could be a lawyer! Yes, definitely a lawyer. They never talked about Harriet that way. She loved to read but often felt like books weren't meant for her, she wasn't meant to read them.

She hadn't seen Amelia for three months, hadn't even spoken to her on the phone. Harriet had asked Dad if she could call her, and he always said it wasn't a good time. Only in recent weeks had she realised that something was about to happen. Mom and Dad were in touch more often. A tense tone, they spoke in low voices on the phone and never seemed to be in agreement. Dad raised his voice now and then, and one time he roared: 'We have to let the kids spend time together!' And now they were on their way.

Did she miss her sister? There were moments with her she missed. Amelia liked to lie on her bed listening to music, and Harriet would stand in the doorway, making herself available. Most of the time Amelia just shouted at Harriet to go away, and Harriet would shout back: 'It's my room too.' But one time her sister invited her in and they lay on the bed together, staring at the ceiling and listening to music Harriet didn't recognise, but which affected her in some peculiar way. Amelia whispered along with the words and Harriet closed her eyes and hoped the album would never end, that it would just keep playing. She missed the moments when it was just her and her sister, the moments when she felt Mom had been wrong all along – they're not night and day, they belong together and they're important to each other.

The highways grew narrower and the woods loomed towards them from either side. Dad had an atlas in his lap, and sometimes he had to stop in the middle of the road to check where he was and where they were going. The yellow glow of the car's indicators illuminated the wall of trees, flowed into the forest through the gaps there. Then they set off again. By the time they arrived it was late at night, a tiny community in the middle of nowhere, a train station and a street of lanterns that looked like moons hanging in a row, and up a hill through the woods, and then they arrived at the house. Mom came outside to greet them. When she breathed, steam blew out of her mouth although it was the middle of summer. Harriet wanted to familiarise herself with the house, but it was difficult to do so in the dark. Two storeys, a bright yellow glow from the windows. Everything else was pitch black. Her parents spoke together softly, and Mom turned to her and brought a hand to her cheek. 'It's so wonderful that you're finally here,' she said. 'You can't tell right now because it's so dark, but there's a lake down there, and we can go swimming tomorrow if you want to.' Mom pointed into the black night and Harriet nodded.

Dad turned around to walk back to the car. 'I'll come pick you up on Sunday,' he said. And he got in the car and she watched as he drove off, listening as the sound of the engine faded in the dark. They went into the house and she looked around the front hall, wondering where Amelia was. Was she in bed already?

'I'll go get a mattress for you,' Mom said, walking off.

The smell of a strange home, a pet of some sort? And all the shoes she didn't recognise in the hall. There was a TV on in another room. She untied her shoes and took her time doing it; it felt good to have something to do. Mom's new boyfriend was standing in the kitchen, loading plates into the dishwasher, and at first it was like he was pretending not to notice that they had company, he just kept working on the dishes. But at last he came over and held up his wet hands to show her why he wasn't shaking her hand. He went back to the dishes. There was something about him, Harriet knew it. Thanks to the phone calls she'd eavesdropped on between her parents, she had come to realise that the boyfriend was somehow part of the problem. One time Dad had snapped into the phone: 'It's not up to him whether the kids get to see each other or not!'

Harriet looked around, discovering familiar objects all around. That chest of drawers that used to be in their hall at home, back when Mom and Dad were together; it still existed back home as a peculiar blank space, its grimy outline left behind on the wall. That chest of drawers was now in this hall, in this home, as though that were perfectly natural. Two leopard-print chairs that Harriet liked to use when she was building a fort, now they were in this strange kitchen. She heard sounds from upstairs. Was that Amelia? Two other children, boys, came quietly down the stairs, noticed her, and hurried back up again.

Mom returned. She handed over a mattress that was cold from a draught and full of weird grown-up stains. Mom showed her the room where she would sleep: an office with a desk and a bookcase full of binders. Mom put sheets on the bare mattress and filled the pillowcases with pillows. 'Is this OK?' she asked.

'Yes,' Harriet said. 'Where's Amelia?'

'She's sleeping,' Mom replied. 'She was too tired to stay up. You'll see her tomorrow.'

Harriet put on her pyjamas and crawled into bed. The mattress was thin and put her close to the rug, which smelled like the dog she still hadn't seen.

Mom sat down on the floor beside her, rested a hand on her cheek. 'I hope this will all go well.'

Harriet took a cautious sniff: Mom's hair smelled like shampoo that belonged to her alone, and when she smelled it she felt butterflies in her stomach.

She woke up early the next day, lay there feeling the floorboards against her back and listening for sounds in the house. The sun blazed beyond the blinds, and her eyes moved over the binders in the bookcase. They were arranged by years, starting with 1971, 1972, 1973, 1974, 1975. After a while someone woke up, she heard the creak of an old door opening, footsteps on the stairs and a tap running in the kitchen. She sneaked into the hall and peered into the kitchen, and Mom was standing there in a robe she'd stolen from the home where she used to live. She was making herself a cup of tea.

When one of the eggs cracked in the pot, she said 'shit' and Harriet had never heard her say that before. She observed her mother as she got breakfast ready, her quick steps between different stations in the kitchen. Who was that person, walking around in there? Harriet didn't recognise the way she moved; she even thought her voice sounded different, shriller. She seemed more anxious here than back home. Harriet had an unpleasant feeling as she imagined that this was probably the real version of Mom. She had pretended to be a mom for all those years, trapped in a home she wanted to escape from, making breakfast for children she didn't want to be a mother to. But here, in this kitchen, she was herself. Harriet watched as she set out plates on the table. This new mom didn't have a very easy time talking to her.

Then they came down one by one. And last of all was Amelia. Harriet decided to look at her a lot this weekend, so she wouldn't forget her face. She thought she should hug her sister when she came down, but Amelia gave no indication that she wanted a hug, and maybe that wasn't unusual; they didn't usually hug each other. Amelia sat down at one end of the table, poured milk into a bowl. Harriet listened to conversations around the table, about people she didn't know, or about things that were foreign to her. She looked at Mom when she was sure Mom wasn't watching, looked at her in secret. Mom was making plans with Amelia about a camp she was going to next week. And about back-to-school shopping. It was so weird and icky somehow, the thought that life would continue there after the weekend, once she was gone. The kitchen became stranger, smells became stronger. One of the boys showed his brother a mouthful of yoghurt to tease him, and they started hitting each other. Mom's new boyfriend shouted at them to stop, and when they didn't listen he grabbed one of them. Mom yelled, things fell on the floor. Harriet didn't notice that Amelia had stood up and was now right beside her. 'Want to go swimming?' she whispered.

They walked down a grassy slope and now she could see the lake, morning-shiny and reflecting the sky. They stood on the wooden dock and gazed down at the muddy bottom, and her sister got a stick and poked it into the sludge to make bubbles come up. Harriet did the same thing, and soon the water was bubbling as if it were carbonated. They took off their clothes and walked into the knee-deep water, and saw tadpoles calmly going about their business, swimming just beneath the surface. They walked out a way, the mud felt nice, offered a little resistance; it was like the bottom of the lake wanted to hold onto Harriet's feet for a moment before it let her move on. Harriet turned to look up the slope at the house. There, on the deck, she spotted Mom, who had settled in to read the morning paper in the morning sun. The two boys pelted out, fighting, it could have been for real or for play. Their cries reached across the lake.

'Those two idiots are such a pain,' Amelia said.

'The short one is cute,' Harriet said. 'Maybe you could go out together.'

Amelia laughed and reached out her hands, turning them

into claws, snapping her hands in the air. 'Now you get the crab,' she said.

Harriet's stomach tickled, a memory of a different lake, a different time, when they lived together as siblings. Harriet shrieked with joy, tried to get away, and Amelia chased her, and the water splashed and their laughter echoed over the quiet lake. They fell all over each other in the green water, and Harriet escaped, but slowly, let herself be caught, because she wanted to feel her sister near.

They wrapped themselves in their towels and sat on the dock. Many times, afterwards, her father interrogated her about what really happened down there by the water's edge, what led up to the disaster. He wanted to know exactly what was said between the sisters and how it could all go so wrong. Harriet refused to tell him, even though Dad wouldn't give in, even though he got mad and shouted at her. She didn't say a peep, and she knew she never would. For her part, she could recount the conversation word for word. She remembers how Amelia turned around and looked at the house, to make sure no one could hear what she was saying. And then she leaned close to Harriet and said she had something to tell her. And Harriet reacted without thinking, without speaking. She simply threw herself on top of her sister, started hitting her in the face. She hammered with her fists and Amelia fended her off with her arms, trying to get hold of her wrists. And then she hit back. Their father had always told them it was OK to fight, but you had to fight fair. This was no fair fight. It got dangerous. They clawed at each other, aiming for the eyes, scratched each other. She remembers Amelia's expression of surprise when she found a big chunk of her sister's hair in her fist. Until at last their towels had fallen off and they were wrestling naked, and Harriet had her sister on her back and Amelia grabbed her by the back of the neck, locked her tight to her chest, and Harriet lay there with her ear pressed close to her sister's heart, heard it beating, and then she bit Amelia's nipple for all she was worth. The nipple came off, ended up in her mouth. It felt like something rubbery between her teeth, she remembers the shock, spitting it onto the dock, how it glistened there in the morning sun. The taste of iron. And everything was quiet and then chaos broke out. Her sister's wild screams; she had never heard anyone scream like that. Amelia lay in a foetal position, holding her chest, and Harriet remembers sitting beside her sister, unable to move, and she saw Mom get up from her chair on the deck and the stone steps outside the door filled with people; Mom's new boyfriend and those boys stood there gaping.

They all dashed at her, down the slope, and when Mom reached them she forced Amelia to uncover her chest and when she saw all the blood she turned to Harriet. 'What have you done?' she screamed. 'Answer me, what have you done?'

Harriet didn't respond the first time she was asked, and not the subsequent times either. Mom pressed the towel to Amelia's wound and her boyfriend searched the dock on all fours for the nipple. At last he found it, held it in his palm. They carried Amelia up the slope, rushed her to the car. They would go to the hospital to sew the nipple back on.

They didn't know then, of course, that it was impossible to sew it back on, that once a nipple has been bitten off it can't be reattached. They carried her off quickly and Amelia was still in shock, screaming with pain.

'You are going home,' Mom called as they stood by the car. 'You are going home this minute!' This was the last thing she said to her. Amelia was led into the car, the two boys hustled into the back, and then they were gone.

Everything was suddenly quiet, only the sounds of the summer, which all seemed strangely enhanced. Birds singing too loudly in the trees, trees creaking eerily in the woods, small rocks rolling towards bigger rocks, she couldn't figure out where. A wind kicked up and the lake rippled before her; she went back up to the house and sat on the ground with her back to the fence to wait for her father. She waited for hours, watching the sun trace its path across the woods. A dog came up and breathed in front of her. It was the animal she'd seen signs of in the house. She leaned over to pet it, but it vanished into the trees. Late that afternoon, she heard the familiar sound of Dad's car beyond the trees. And as evening approached they drove back towards Stockholm. And all the while she kept the promise she'd made to herself: she wouldn't tell, and at last Dad got tired of asking the same question without getting a response, and it was finally quiet in the car. Not even the radio was on, just the sound of the dull engine and the sudden whoosh as an oncoming car flashed by. It got late and twilight fell, the sun flickering between the trees, and she kept herself awake, didn't fall asleep even once as they silently rode into the night, and in that silence she knew, she knew even then, that from now on she was on the run, she had to leave everything else behind, now it was just her and Dad.

The train stops at a station in a city that looks deserted. A whistle far down the platform and they start moving again, out into the summer. Dad gets up, says he has to pee, and she takes the opportunity to ask if he can get her backpack down, because she wants to draw the meadows outside the window, and he gives it to her. She watches him as he walks off, the train rocks a bit and Dad has to hold onto a headrest. A thought – Dad is old – comes and goes, but then it lingers somewhere. She opens the backpack and takes out her case of markers and pad of paper. At the bottom of the backpack she sees the urn. She sees the little cross on its lid, which would also serve as a handle if you wanted to open it. She carefully takes the urn out and holds it in her arms. It's pale grey, and its surface is rough like sandpaper. She rests one hand along its side, thinks that it still feels warm, as if there were glowing coals that hadn't yet faded. But it's probably just her imagination – the urn has been in the hall for a long time. She places it on the table in front of her. When she leans towards it and looks up close, the cross looks very large. She takes out her markers and draws a summer meadow, and above the meadow she puts clouds, white and high, and in one corner of the drawing she puts a flock of birds under a bright yellow sun. In the middle of the field she draws a large cross, with Jesus nailed to it.

72

'Oh my God, what are you doing?' Dad says.

He's standing in the aisle and his small eyes are wide. 'Put that away this minute,' he says.

She hurries to put the urn in the backpack and Dad takes it from her. He places the backpack on the hat rack and sinks back into his seat. The blood pulses faster through her body, she feels hot and stupid. And the train is moving fast now, it's no longer possible to see any details through the window, everything is blurry with speed; they thunder through the world, only getting faster. Sharp sounds just outside the body of the train, creaks and squeals and howls. Is the train supposed to go this fast? Her markers rattle against one another, slide along the table, she has to hold onto them to keep them from falling to the floor. She sees the drawing before her, the summer meadow and the sun and the birds and Jesus on the cross, with two black dots for eyes and a mouth like a line. The thin, black lip-line makes a smile. A mean smile.

Chapter 6

Yana

Her seat is next to the lavatory, and right away a line forms next to her: three, four, five people waiting to take their morning pee. She gets out the photo album and places it in her lap. She wants to be alone with the pictures, but it feels like everyone who needs to pee is crowding her. The passengers' full bladders are at face-height for her, their urine so very close. She gets up from her seat and walks away. She enters a quiet car and there sit the two conscripts she saw on the platform before boarding the train. They've stretched out their long legs under the table between them, their heavy boots lying every which way. One has red hair. 'Is this seat free?' she asks.

'Sure,' one says, quickly scooping up the belongings he'd placed on the seat beside him. She sits down, the seat is worn and she can feel the metal through the fabric. The guys squint out at the landscape but don't know what to do with their eyes once the train enters a tunnel. The rock walls screech through the open windows.

'Are you in the quiet car because you want to be left alone?' she asks.

'Oh, no,' says the redhead. 'We didn't book the tickets; we don't know why we ended up here.'

'Aha. So that means I don't have to be completely quiet here.'

The redhead laughs. 'Oh, no,' he says again.

She crosses her legs, has to help her thigh along; with a sudden motion she lifts her knee in both hands to settle it in place across the other knee. She notices that the two conscripts watch this happen. She reads their eyes, knows everything about them. They may be discreet, but she always sees them: the corners of eyes take note that she's fat.

She used to work as a safety ambassador in the subway, and she didn't like her job for that very reason, that instant when people she encountered quickly eyed her body up and down and then pretended they hadn't seen anything out of the ordinary. During night shifts they weren't as subtle about it, of course; sometimes drunk teenagers shouted at her as she passed. At last she asked to be assigned a different job, and they offered her the ticket booth at Hägerstensåsen subway station. She likes it better there, feels protected in her booth, her thighs hidden beneath the desk.

The psychologist said she has to break out of her loneliness, has to make an effort to talk to other people. But it's so hard. She's never been a talker. She was struck by a realisation one

Sunday a few weeks ago – she hadn't used her voice all week-end. Not a syllable had escaped her mouth for forty-eight hours. She lay in bed that night and tested her voice, uttering long vowels into her dark bedroom. The other day she was standing in line at the grocery store and as the woman ahead of her went to pay she realised she'd forgotten her wallet. For a second she wasn't sure what to do, but then she turned to Yana: 'Sorry, could you pay for this for me and I can Swish you the amount?'

Yana had been paralysed.

'I forgot my wallet,' said the woman. Yana had begun to stammer; for some reason she didn't want to help, but she didn't know why. She had the idea that it might be some sort of monkey business. Someone behind her in line called, 'You can Swish me.' And they had begun to tap at their phones, making chit-chat, easily, without any trouble. It was so simple, and the woman disappeared and Yana stood there just feeling stupid.

When she was little and the TV flickered, she would often imitate her father, slam her fist into its top, delivering hard blows to make it magically start working again, until she gave up and turned it off, with an intrusive thought that wouldn't leave her alone: what if there's nothing wrong with the TV, what if it was her eyes? That was how she was starting to look at her surroundings these days. Maybe it wasn't that other people are weird; maybe it was just the way she was looking at them.

She glances at the two young men sitting beside her and

takes out the photo album and places it on the table before her. 'Where are you stationed?' she asks.

'Linköping.'

'Linköping,' she repeats. 'I'm going further west, to Malma Station,' she says.

'What are you doing there?'

'Well, as it happens,' she says, 'it's a pretty interesting story.'

One of them fiddles with the beret he's taken off and put in his lap. And Yana starts to tell the tale, recounting events so casually that she's surprised at first. Maybe her calmness has to do with their alert eyes, their friendly smiles. They're curious about what she has to say, she can feel the connection she's making and it gives her strength.

She starts at the beginning. She was a little girl back then, she says, and a circus had come to town. When her father took her to school early each morning she watched it slowly taking shape up at Gärdet. They built an enclosure for the horses and another for the elephants. Poles were set in the ground; the popcorn stand was constructed. She had talked so much about the circus with her parents. Surely she didn't actually dare to ask if she could go, but they must have noticed how much she wanted to. One day, Mom and Dad's relationship took a nosedive. Their fights on that day were worse than ever; they said things they'd never before said to each other, unforgiveable things, things they couldn't take back. She sat in her room, listening as they shouted at each other. In the midst of all the turmoil, her parents disappeared. They were going to take a walk, they said, and when they came back that afternoon they stood in the doorway to her bedroom. Mom held red tickets in her hand, waving them near her face as if to cool off. Reconciled and full of guilt, perhaps, they had decided to let Yana go to the circus for the first time in her life. She put on a red dress and allowed Mom to brush the rats' nests out of her hair, and all three of them walked through the mild evening. It was still warm out although the sun had set, because there was something wrong with that summer: it lasted into the autumn, it was hot every day.

She could see the spotlights from far off, and as she grew closer she could also smell candy floss, animal droppings and hay. The big top was so white it was almost blue, and it was anchored to the ground. They walked past a long line of wagons and caravans and Dad told her the circus artistes lived in them. She thought it looked romantic and pictured how the performers would sit before fires each evening, still wearing silver clothes and heavy make-up, how they would drink wine and sing, the night still young and with many hours left before the next show. To her this seemed like freedom.

Mom had bought tickets for the best seats, right by the ring. This had annoyed Dad. You can see just as well from the bleachers, so why pay that kind of money? But that was who she was, Mom, always determined to live a life she couldn't afford; Yana imagines that's how she could stand being herself, or living the life she had ended up in. Seated above them in the bleachers was a gang of teenagers who had brought beer along. And all around her she hardly heard anyone speaking Swedish. Most of them seemed to be

German. A clown came in and used only sounds to communicate, pig-like squeals. The sounds frightened her, it was like he had forgotten language and only had these noises left. The music seemed jarring and crooked, and it was playing too loudly on the crappy loudspeakers. And in the silence between numbers, she heard shrill sounds from anxious animals backstage, animals that were trapped and wanted out. Grotesque howling outside the tent, which sounded like wires snapping in the dark. A man wearing a white suit and a cold smile came out with a monkey on his shoulder for the next act. The monkey was wearing a gold vest and kept slipping away from his owner. The man took out a ball and threw it to the monkey, and when he asked for it back the monkey simply tossed it in a different direction and it landed in the sawdust in the middle of the ring, and the audience gave a surreal round of applause, as if they were actors. The man picked up the ball and threw it back to the monkey, who caught it, and then the animal turned towards the bleachers and threw it into the audience.

'And it wasn't as if I wanted to catch it,' Yana said to the conscripts. 'But the ball was coming straight for me.'

So she stood up and caught it.

'A perfect catch, the audience clapped. And the man in white started calling for me to throw it back to the monkey, and I just stood there. It was like I was paralysed.'

Yana picks up the container of *snus* that's on the table and imitates herself, bewildered and holding the *snus* in her right hand.

'The ball was made of rubber, it was heavier than you would have thought. And it had a texture, a zigzag pattern I still remember precisely, and the man shouted at me in English to throw the ball. "Throw the ball! Throw the ball!"'

Out of nowhere, a spotlight was on her and she was blinded by its sharp beam. Mom was exhilarated to be at the centre of attention. She shook Yana and hissed at her to throw the ball back, the incomprehensible urging of the Germans grew closer, and the colours grew stronger, bright alarm colours everywhere, as if the big top were trying to warn her. She looked up into the skies of the circus tent, saw the shiny helium balloons that kids had lost, now caught there. 'Throw the ball!' shouted the man in white.

So she threw it.

'The ball hit the monkey on the head. It fell and lay there twitching, almost lifeless. The man in the white suit dashed over to the monkey, and others ran up too, they came out of the wings and gathered around the animal. And the Germans in the bleachers shouted, "You killed the monkey!" Mom and Dad got up and started tugging at me, they said we were going home right that minute. I cried, I couldn't see the way out through all my tears.'

They hurried home through the black September night, and her parents didn't say a word. It was muggy out, and as they crossed the field the starry sky was low above their heads. When they got home, they told her to brush her teeth and go to bed.

'I lay there in bed, trying to fall asleep. Mom and Dad started arguing and shouting again. The fight lasted for ages, longer than usual. And then it was quiet. Suddenly Mom opened the door to my room and stood in the doorway for a moment. When she saw that I was awake, she took a few steps towards me, stood in the centre of the room. She reached out her arm. "I'm wearing your bracelet," she whispered, and she showed me the jewellery I had made for her, blue and pink beads. "I will wear it always," she said. When I woke up the next morning they were gone.'

She looks up at the guys.

'Later that night, Dad came back without Mom.'

Yana rests a hand on the photo album. Its cover has been warmed by the rays of sun that are falling through the window. 'My dad never told me what happened, Mom was just gone, but all through my childhood I was absolutely convinced it was my fault. I thought she chose not to come back because she was angry at me for killing the monkey.' She laughs, looks down at the table. 'And Dad did nothing to explain it to me, not once did he say the only thing I wanted to hear: it wasn't your fault. Not once did we talk about what happened that day.'

She runs her hand slowly back and forth across the pleather.

'But then Dad died a few weeks ago. And yesterday I found this in his apartment.'

She opens it to the first page. The delicate cellophane has yellowed; beneath it the shapes of the photographs, and Yana feels her heart pounding. It's so silly, coincidence is, yet what great things it can set in motion. The hair on her arm stands up as she takes in the dark squares behind the thin paper. 'This photo album is from 1976. And the minute I saw the first picture—'

'Excuse me . . .' says the redhead.

She looks up at him.

'This is super-interesting,' he says. He leans towards her, lowers his voice a notch. 'But the two of us were out partying yesterday, because it was our last day of leave. We didn't get much sleep. I think we need to get some shut-eye before we arrive.'

She looks at the redhead, then at the other guy. Now she can see the glances they're exchanging, and realises that those looks have been there throughout this conversation. One of them turns to the window and gazes out with a small smile on his lips. She closes the photo album and puts it in her bag. She stands up and walks away.

Chapter 7

Oskar

Oskar's phone vibrates; the screen says 'YANA'. Oskar silences the phone and lets it ring. The screen blinks nervously for a moment, then goes dark. He looks out. The train has just stopped at yet another station and the sounds of a small town find their way into the car through the open windows. A guy on a skateboard goes by on the street, and it sounds like a gunshot each time he misses a trick. A feeble breeze takes hold of a few flagpoles on the square, their nylon cables sluggishly smacking the wood. A lawn mower is running a few hedges away. And there's a similar sound, but closer, Oskar's phone again, the vibration launching it on a journey along the table. He picks it up, the screen says 'YANA'. He rejects the call and puts the phone down.

He bought two cups of tea in the buffet car and tries to take a sip, but it's still too hot. How can they serve such scalding beverages? His phone rings yet again, 'YANA', and he silences it again. He probably should pick up, but he doesn't know what to say to her. She must be a wreck after everything that happened yesterday. And then she woke up this morning to discover that her parents were gone. He can tell all of this is having an effect on her. And she hears and sees everything. In the middle of an argument a feeling sometimes comes over Oskar, he'll fall silent and look over at the hall to find a shadow there, listening, and then she disappears into her room. She's been spending a lot of time in there recently. On some afternoons there's no sign of her at all. She comes out when he calls her to the table, eats without a word, and disappears to her room again. They say 'hi' ever more infrequently when he gets home from work. The other day, Oskar peeked into Yana's room to find her sitting quietly in her window seat, crying. Her mascara had run. He didn't even know that she used make-up; when had she started doing that? Was it normal for an eleven-year-old?

'Are you OK?' he'd asked.

'I'm fine.'

'Were you crying?'

'No.'

And that was all she said. She just looked at him and he wracked his brains for something to say, something that would bring them closer together, but he couldn't think of what that might be.

When do you know you've lost a child? There must not be one particular moment, it's the sort of thing that happens in small steps, strange little shifts, hardly noticeable. But certainly there must be a starting point, a sudden distance. A gap between parent and child, and once it's there, the breakdown can only continue. Because it wasn't there from the start, right? Or was it? A late-night conversation in their kitchen, ages ago. He and Harriet lived in that cramped apartment, he owned a single suit that he put on each morning before heading out to show the firm's lowest-priority properties. Yana was ten months old at the time, a little baby who didn't make a sound all day but screamed at night. They always joked about that: as she lay there quietly in her stroller they would say she was gathering strength for the night. It was a cold night, January outside the window, it was that winter that seemed unusually dark; when they went out on the balcony they could sometimes see the Milky Way, it was so tangible, like a silver tunnel between worlds. They'd invited a childhood friend of Oskar's over. His name was Joakim, but people called him Bornholm because he'd once bought a cottage on the island of Bornholm. He sold the place after a few years, but the nickname stuck. And they sat around long after dinner, opening fresh bottles of wine, and then Yana woke up again. She was always so sudden about it, zero to a hundred, never a soft whimper, just straight to chaos. Oskar and Harriet heard her howl and both of them looked down at the ashtray. He whispered, 'I can't ...' She stood up with a sigh that was more resigned than annoyed, and went to put the baby back to sleep.

'She's sure got pipes,' Bornholm said with a laugh.

'It goes right through the walls,' Oskar replied.

Bornholm studied him intently, lowered his voice. 'I think she wants closeness.'

'Yeah,' said Oskar. And then a few seconds of silence. 'Wait, what do you mean?'

'Touch her,' Bornholm replied. 'Hold her as much as you can.'

Oskar laughed. 'I do,' he said. 'We do.'

'Yeah,' said Bornholm, and they didn't say anything and the shadowy light played tricks on his appearance, the frames of his glasses flowing down his temples. 'When we get together with the kids in the park and grill hotdogs,' Bornholm said. 'I notice you always leave her in her stroller.'

'Well, she's sleeping,' Oskar said.

'But haven't you thought about it?' he whispered. 'Everyone else picks up their kid. But you two don't touch her. I honestly don't know if I've ever seen you hold her.'

Oskar smiled and shook his head, and this audacity slipped into him as stealthily as poison, and the room grew smaller, that kitchen, their first kitchen, where you could see a sliver of the sea between the concrete buildings, the warm, wide floorboards, the table full of wine bottles that cast towering shadows on the walls, and he took out his Marlboros and Yana only screamed louder from the next room and he heard Harriet's muffled shushing and lulling, and they sat in that kitchen in silence, and Oskar shook his head again and smiled slightly as he looked at his cigarette. 'I think you should go now,' said Oskar.

'But, Oskar—' said Bornholm.

'What the fuck are you trying to say?' Oskar said and bolted to his feet and began to clear the plates.

Bornholm stood up too, tried to say something more, and when he got no response he began to help with the dishes.

'I swear,' Oskar said. 'If you don't leave this minute I don't know what I'll do.'

Their farewell was brief, and later that night, once Oskar had washed the dishes and they were undressing for bed, he went to Yana's crib and looked down at her as she slept, her tiny ribcage heaving beneath her sleepsuit. He picked her up and lay down with her in bed.

'What are you doing?' Harriet whispered.

'Let's let her sleep with us for a while.'

And he lay with his daughter right next to him. He brought his nose to her head and smelled a scent he hadn't smelled before, peach but more, harder to capture, and he wondered if it could be the laundry softener in her clothes. But as he inhaled with his nose to her soft hair, he realised it was simply what babies' heads smell like. And he lay close to her that night, felt her warm body against his own, and he knew that he would never let go of her now.

When do you lose a child? Yana learned to speak early, but quickly stopped again. She's a real observer! That's what they always said about her, and they still do. Always as though this were an admirable trait, as if it made her a little better than other children. She isn't a loud and rambunctious kind of kid, no, she registers and notices instead, meticulously learning about the world, gathering information that might turn out to be useful. Sometimes he feels desperate when he sees her just standing there and taking it all in. This isn't how it's supposed to be, surely? Isn't a kid *supposed* to play? When did she stop taking part in her own childhood?

This silence between him and Yana, when did it begin? She's always on guard. Once he was standing in the kitchen, peeling potatoes, and Yana came in. 'How are you feeling, Dad?' she asked. 'You look sad.' He assured her that he wasn't sad at all. After she'd left, he said to Harriet: 'She's always so considerate.' At that, Harriet leaned forward, whispered, 'Have you ever heard her ask me how I'm feeling, or tell me I look sad?'

'No,' he replied. 'What do you mean?'

'She doesn't ask me how I'm feeling or whether I'm happy or sad, because she doesn't keep track of my moods. She's not afraid of me.'

He had bought Yana a backpack for her first day of school, pink with white rabbits, and in the outer pocket they packed a pencil case, scented erasers and a ruler. On their walk to school she said nothing, she just walked with great focus, gazing down at the pavement her hand in his damp and cool. All the pupils were gathered in the schoolyard and the teachers had signs to help the children sort themselves into their classes. Yana's teacher gave her a helium balloon, which she was supposed to release at a given moment to signify the start of school. The other kids dashed around, being kids, but Yana just stood there by his side, pressing her shoulder to Oskar's hip. And the principal stood on the stone steps and gave a speech that partially vanished into the breeze, and then she called to the children to release their balloons, and Oskar had to tell Yana to let go, and a buzz of excitement passed through the crowd as the balloons rose and grew smaller against the blue sky. 'You have to look,' he said to her, trying to get her to shift her gaze from the ground. 'You have to look at the balloons, Yana!'

The other parents said goodbye to their children, disappeared into cars and were gone, and he kneeled to stroke her cheek. 'Honey, I know you're nervous, but it's going to be OK.'

She looked down and nodded, and tears sprang to her eyes. 'I don't want you to go,' she said.

'What if I come with you to your classroom? We can say goodbye there instead.'

They entered the school, up the stone stairs with their fossil impressions that came from the earth's beginning, and the sun shone in through the high windows and struck the white walls of the corridor. Her teacher was standing by the door, watching the children as they came into the classroom, with her bunch of keys and the same grin as she'd been wearing in the schoolyard just now, and Yana's resistance increased the closer they came. And he exchanged a look with the teacher and she nodded in understanding, went to stand by the lectern. He bent down to Yana and said it was time, and she started to cry again, more audibly this time, and Oskar said, 'OK, you have to go in now.' She squeezed him tight around the neck, he tried to loosen her grip. 'You really have to go now,' he whispered, and she squeezed tighter. 'No, Daddy, please.'

'Come on.'

'Please, Daddy.'

'OK, fine,' he said, standing up suddenly. 'We'll leave.' He took her arm and pulled her brusquely into the corridor. Insistent steps towards the exit, and then she changed her mind. 'No, Dad. I'm brave. I'm brave enough now.' They tugged at one another, pulling in opposite directions; now she wanted to go back to the classroom and he wanted to take her out to the schoolyard. He was stronger, of course, and she was dragged along in his anger, crying, her protests growing increasingly desperate. 'Please, Daddy,' she said. 'I'm not afraid any more, I'll be OK.'

'Just stop it,' he snapped as they came to the stairwell.

'I'm OK now,' she cried. 'I promise, Daddy. I'll be OK.'

'But you don't want to!'

'I want to now!'

'And I don't have time for this,' he said, and he stopped and grabbed her by the shoulders and shouted, 'Because I have to go to work!'

'I can go in now!' she shouted back.

He dragged her onward, away from the school. He sat down with her on a bench by a fountain, and it was only there, once they'd sat quietly for a while before the little waterfall, that he understood what he'd done, and he saw her worried gaze and the long hair that was stuck to her cheeks by her tears. They regarded one another.

'Sorry,' she said.

'No, don't say you're sorry. I'm the one who was being stupid,' he replied.

He hugged her, felt her body through her light down coat, and the fountain thundered in front of them. 'You know what,' he said. 'Let's forget this and go eat some cake.'

They went to a café and he got a coffee and ordered her a piece of princess cake, and he observed the way she bolted it down, with no enjoyment, finishing it in just a few minutes, and he realised she was eating so fast because she was anxious, about him and his lack of time. She got up. 'Let's go, Dad. I can do it now.'

Once he'd dropped her off and was back on the street, he realised he still had her backpack slung over his shoulder, and he walked along with bunnies on his back, and he didn't know where to go. He aimlessly strolled the streets around the school. He sat down on the same bench where they'd sat earlier and gazed at the flowing water. He opened his daughter's bag, the rattle of the pencil case carrying so many memories from his own childhood. He took out the erasers and sniffed them. One of them was shaped like a peach, and when he brought it to his nose it reminded him of that time long ago when he'd lain with his baby in bed, smelling her head. And he buried his head in the white rabbits.

Once you've lost your child, what do you do to get them back? The other day he looked in on her and she was lying on the bed and listening to music with a bowl of crisps on her belly, and he sat down on the edge of the bed beside her and they listened together for a while, he ate a few crisps, asked a few questions, which she answered briefly, but otherwise she just lay there stiff and unspeaking, waiting for him to leave. Always silent. The observer! All her secrets. Harriet, of course, has even more. They're so similar, Yana and Harriet, and yet so different. Yana keeps her secrets through silence; Harriet by way of lies.

That's where they always land, at couples' therapy, in her lies. Harriet is clever, but she can't get away with them because he has ample evidence of her untruths, and when he lays them out before a third party it's devastating for her. The therapist urged them to have an 'honesty night' with each other. 'You should drink some wine, just the two of you, and have an open and honest conversation about things you've previously had difficulty discussing.' That night, he bought shrimp at the market hall and they opened a bottle of wine, and she had put on make-up and was wearing shoes indoors, and he felt silly sitting there in his socks and the whole situation seemed off and he was nervous somehow. 'So what should we talk about?' he asked, and they didn't say anything and picked at the shrimp, until she raised her eyes to look at him. 'We can talk about something you never want to say a word about,' she said.

'What's that?'

'Who we had sex with before we met.'

He laughed, shook his head. 'You're crazy,' he said.

'No, it's not crazy. There's no danger in talking about it.'

'Maybe not, but that's not what the therapist meant when she asked us to have an honest conversation.'

'I think it's an excellent example of just that. We aren't supposed to have secrets from each other.'

'But I don't want to know how many people you've had sex with.'

'But I do.'

He laughed. 'You're crazy,' he said again.

And so they began to tell each other, even though he really didn't want to. Every other time they had raised the topic of former lovers, it had ended poorly. Harriet started by recounting the time she lost her virginity, and then it was his turn. They worked forwards chronologically and it went better than he'd feared, these events had taken place so long ago that they seemed harmless. They laughed at themselves and each other, refilled their wine glasses, and when he was finished with his, she had a lot left to account for, and they laughed at that too. She described most of the sex she'd had as disastrous, probably as a kindness to him, and it worked, the evening felt light-hearted and the wine made him soft and sentimental. He watched her as she pulled her hair down in front of her eyes when she said something she was ashamed of. But then something in her tone shifted. No one else would have noticed, but having lived with her for so long, it caught his attention at once. She was telling a story about a man named Harry. It took place at a train station. She was heading home and arrived at the station early, so she went to a deli. It was one of those places where the cashier calls your name when the food is ready, and when they called Harriet's name she went to get her coffee, and there stood a man who was trying to claim the same order. After some confusion they figured out that she was Harriet and he was Harry, their names so similar that they each thought their name had been called. He asked if he could join her. So they sat down at her table, and he suggested they grab a beer instead. She watched him as he went to the register to pay. She loved this about life. A new direction. And outside the train station the sun moved lower in the sky and people walked by faster as the afternoon rush began. She couldn't describe it, she said. The feeling that everything was right. They had a few more beers, and of course she lost track of time. Suddenly she looked at her watch in surprise. 'I missed my train,' she said.

'There's something between us, isn't there,' he said.

'Hmm,' she said, drinking with a smile. 'I have to go to the bathroom.' She got up and took a few steps, then turned back towards him and said, 'Harry and Harriet.'

When she came out of the bathroom, he was just standing there outside her door, waiting for her. She pulled him into the stall and they kissed. There wasn't much room, and when he was about to enter her he lifted her onto the sink. She didn't remember the details, the sink detached from the wall and she tumbled to the floor and hit her head on a hook. It left a gash above her eyebrow. He used paper towels to stop the bleeding. And she looked at her watch and said, 'Shit, I can't miss another train,' and that's where they parted ways, she took one of the bloody paper towels and wrote her phone number on it and dashed off, hurrying over the platforms, adrenaline streaming through her body and her pulse throbbing in her wound, and she ran until she found the train to Stockholm and without a valid ticket, and with hardly a single krona in her pocket, she hopped on.

'And there, onboard that train,' she said to him, picking up a shrimp and slowly peeling it. 'That's where I met you.'

He gazed at her in wonder as she told the tale, and it was as though time was slowing down the further in the story she got, until at last he could hardly hear her, she was only making unpleasant sounds. And then, silence.

'Stop,' he said. 'Just stop your fucking games.'

She laughed. 'It's no game.'

He looked down at his plate. The candle was flickering anxiously, a window was open somewhere. The wine glass was oily and the room was dim with cigarette smoke. And he knew that from that moment on, the story of how Harriet and Oskar met would not begin on a train to Stockholm, but at a bar in Gothenburg Central Station.

'You're so cheap,' he said softly. She looked at him, perplexed, and he couldn't tell if it was an act or if she was genuinely surprised by his reaction. 'Cheap like a whore.'

He rose from the kitchen table but stopped mid-motion, cocking an ear towards the hall. The apartment was perfectly silent, yet he'd heard something. 'Yana?' he said.

'Yeah?' he heard her say from the darkness.

'Go to bed.'

Yana silently retreated to her room, and there was a tiny click as she closed the door behind her.

When do you lose your daughter?

Oskar's phone rings again, vibrating against the pale table-top. It's Yana again, and this time he decides to answer, for one instant he sees it all clearly, he knows exactly what he'll say to her. He understands how it has to go now, he knows what to do, and he feels a weightlessness like when he was young; there's a solution to everything and it's only seconds away. But his insight is gone as quickly as it came, everything grows murky again, words flowing out, melting into one another. He lets the phone ring, and when it stops he stares at the screen.

'Who was it?'

Harriet has woken up, and she's gazing at him vacantly.

'Yana.'

'Why didn't you answer?'

'There's no point,' he says. 'It'll only cut out. The coverage here is a joke.'

He gazes out at the empty platform. This is one of those stations that hardly ever gets to participate, most of the trains just pass through without stopping, whizzing on to more relevant places. But this train is making an honest attempt to let people on and off. He sees the back of a conductor just outside the window, his gaze sweeping the empty platform patiently, as though he's sure the passengers are hiding around here somewhere, he just has to find them.

'It doesn't feel right to leave Yana home alone,' he says. 'I'm worried about her.'

'Yeah,' she replies. 'But she'll be OK. I told her she could go down to see Åkeby any time she wanted.'

Åkeby was their downstairs neighbour, a retiree Yana had taken a liking to. He had a cocker spaniel and sometimes the two of them took the dog on walks together.

'Please,' he says. 'Can't you tell me what we're doing here?'

She catches sight of the paper cup and places her hands around it, as though she wanted to warm up. 'We're going to a place I've wanted to show you for a long time.'

He nods, gazes out of the window. The station looks like a whipped-cream confection keeping vigil over the platform with its shadow. He notices that she's bent towards him, is gesturing at him to come closer. She lowers her voice. 'You know the monkey yesterday,' she says. 'I can't stop thinking about it. She threw the ball so hard. It was like . . .'

He closes his eyes.

'It was like she wanted to kill it.'

Someone blows a whistle and the train sets off again. No one got off; no one got on. All the vast amounts of energy it takes to stop a big train, for nothing. They pull out of the station and are soon in the forest. He can't see the sky, only fir trees growing too close to the tracks. The train gathers speed, the sun flashing increasingly rapid signals between the trees, blinking at him like a mysterious code, and he brings the paper cup to his lips and just as he's about to take a sip he inhales deeply, and he smells the tropical fruits, and then the slow emergence of something else, the deep and distant scent of peach.

Chapter 8

Harriet

She looks for signs that they've arrived, for Dad to collect himself, or for him to stare eagerly out of the window. But he's just sitting there; he takes out another cigarette. A faint haze has appeared in the car, lots of people smoking here, but no one smokes as prettily as Dad does, the cigarette so far out on his fingertips that it looks like he'll drop it at any moment. He smokes half and stubs it out in the metal ashtray; he always does that, gets sick of it after a while. He takes off his glasses and closes his eyes, and then she can watch him in peace and quiet. His checked shirt unbuttoned and the skin of his chest white and pebbled like a chicken's. His sleeves were rolled up, a glimpse of the tattoo on his right arm visible: it's an eagle, and its wings encircle his arm like a band. He always says that's why he became a photographer, to get close to the eagles; he does the advertising work to make money, he says, but he lives for the eagles. Whenever he comes home late at night he's almost always been out at the nature reserve. He heads straight for the darkroom, the rolls of film in their plastic cases clattering against each other in that jacket that has all sorts of pockets. And after a few hours the contours would show up, the blank paper would come to life. Harriet often stood in the hall watching Dad as he bent over his photographs. She looked at him while he looked at the eagles.

The first thing Dad did after Mom and Amelia moved out was redo the dining room. He hung cloth over the windows, a curtain over the door, and on the dining room table he placed basins containing the different fluids. It made Harriet nervous. How is the family supposed to reunite now that Dad has transformed the room where they eat meals together? Sometimes when Dad was gone she would go in there, the red light always glowing, the sharp odours of the fluids in their steel basins. The glass cabinet with the plates and silverware was still there. It was like a dark red monument to their lives. It felt like the point of the room was to use it, on occasion, to grieve.

Dad hung the photographs like clothes on a line and then laid them on the table in the kitchen. Hundreds of pictures of eagles, always so far away you could never see much of anything beyond a vague black spot. For some of them he had used one of the long lenses, which meant the eagles were closer, but in some way even more distant. Those ones reminded her of the grainy pictures she sometimes saw in the newspaper, from people who claimed to have spotted a

UFO. Each of Dad's expeditions was a failure; he came home and stormed into the darkroom with an energy that slowly drained away. He never got close enough to the birds. Still, he saved every photo in an album, which Harriet loved to page through. It made her feel calm to look at the blurry pictures. Nothing but black dots, no information. Harriet liked everything that was far away. She used to be interested in space, learning all the constellations by heart and reading the remarkably dazzling stories of how they had come to be. When she turned six, she got a telescope for her birthday. Dad set it up in her room, pointing it at the moon. But she got too close, now she could see its surface so near, the craters and the vast deserts. She couldn't look through the telescope any more; it was unbearable to know that the moon really existed.

Only once had Harriet herself seen an eagle, on a walk with Dad. Dad stopped and placed a hand on her shoulder. 'Look at that guy,' he whispered. Far off, at the edge of a large meadow, in the top of a tree, she saw the bird. They began to walk towards it, but after just a few steps it unfolded its wings and took off.

'He saw us,' Dad said.

'How could he?' Harriet asked. 'His back was to us.'

'He could feel us coming.'

Later on, Harriet thought a lot about that eagle: it seems to her that her father is like an eagle, hearing and seeing everything she does. Even when he's sitting with his back to her in the kitchen, bent over a bowl of cereal, it's like he can still see her. He takes note of every move she makes, but he doesn't interfere, just sits quietly and eats his cereal.

Mom once said that she thought Dad loved animals more than people. Maybe that was why the rabbit was so important to him as well. A few weeks after Harriet's fight with Amelia, Dad said they were going for a car ride, and they headed for the suburbs, balconies like little boxes with a view of the highway, hundreds of satellite dishes on the building façade, all pointing at the same vague point in space. They rang a doorbell on the first floor and a woman opened the door, led them straight to a boy's room, and on the bed lay a guy a few years older than her, reading a comic book.

'They're taking the rabbit now,' the mom said in a voice that almost sounded accusatory, and the guy nodded.

A cage on the floor, full of straw and two small houses. 'OK, so here's Lasagne,' she said. But there was no rabbit to be seen, the mom lifted one of the houses and, with a little giggle said, 'Nope,' when she didn't find the rabbit there. She lifted the other house, and there was the animal, cowering, trying to hide in the straw.

Harriet moved closer. He had brown fur with white spots on his back, and long ears that were pressed back along his body for the moment. He held perfectly still, his black pupils gleaming with fear. The mom picked up the rabbit with one hand, so his back legs dangled in the air.

'Do you want to hold him?' she asked. 'Might be best to sit down.' The mom placed the rabbit on her lap and Harriet gingerly stroked his back.

'His name is Lasagne?' Harried asked softly.

'Yes,' the mom replied. 'Jonas thought he looked like lasagne, so that's what we called him, right, Jonas?'

'Yeah,' said the guy on the bed, without looking up from his comic book.

The mom told them how to take care of the rabbit, how to refill the water and what food he should eat. It was hard for Harriet to listen because he was in her lap now, this tiny animal, almost weightless, and when she held his ribcage she could feel his heart beating fast, and for the first time she felt that she was approaching something greater than herself, an enormous responsibility that bordered on power. It was up to her now to keep him alive.

Dad took a wad of cash from the tight pocket of his jeans and Harriet tried to see what the rabbit cost, but it happened too fast and she didn't have time. As they left, Dad carried the cage and she carried the rabbit. On the way out of the room, Harriet stopped next to the boy. 'I promise . . . ' she said, and he glanced up from his comic book. It was just the two of them in the room now; she could hear the mom conversing with Dad out in the hall. 'I promise to take good care of him.'

'OK,' he said. He sat up in bed, smiled at her. 'Great.'

When the rabbit first arrived home, he was scared and slunk along the walls of his cage, staring into the corner. Nothing unusual there; he'd been taken from his home and put in a dark box for the ride to their place. When they placed the cage in her room, Dad said she should be cautious with him, that she should let the rabbit come to her. She opened the door of the cage and lay down on her back nearby to wait. It took a long time, but at last he was brave enough to come out. He padded around cautiously, the tiny scraping sounds as he hopped across the floor. And he gently began to nose at her, and she lay on her side and he came up to her face and licked her chin. His rough tongue, which almost caught on the point of her chin. After that, the rabbit was never afraid of her again, it was him and her.

That night, Dad came into her room with a collar to put around the rabbit's neck. It had a little wooden tag where he wrote Harriet's name. 'It means that the two of you belong together,' he said.

The next evening, she stood outside Dad's room, hesitating for a long time before she went in. She knocked softly on the doorless frame. Dad was lying on the left side of the big double bed, as though he were saving the right side for Mom, as though she would come back. 'I thought a lot about it,' she said. 'And I was wondering if I could change the rabbit's name.'

'Don't you like Lasagne?'

'No. I feel sorry for him, having that name.'

Dad laughed. He looked up at the ceiling. 'Of course you can change his name.'

'I can?'

'Definitely. Call him whatever you want.'

'Then I want him to be called Ninen.'

'Good, then that's his name.'

Autumn came and every day was just like the last. When

she got home from school she ran to her room. She cleaned the cage, refilled food and water. That autumn was her best one ever, because it was the autumn when everything happened with Dad. Typically, he went straight to the darkroom when he got home, and when he came out he was dizzy from the fumes and lay down in bed and wasn't himself for the rest of the evening. That autumn, though, he went to Harriet's room instead, lay down with her on the floor to play with the rabbit, lay there on his belly beside her and extended a finger to the rabbit. 'Little guy,' he said in his strained voice. She felt the heat of Dad's body as they lay close. And when they got out the rabbit and took turns holding him, she felt his soft hands on hers, she could get to know them in peace and quiet, always a little warmer than her own, softer than any other hands she'd known. Their touches were like tiny jolts, bolts of lightning inside her. She didn't understand why her heart beat harder each time they touched.

One night, just before bed, Harriet called out for Dad, who promptly appeared in the doorway. She asked him to come in and lie down on his back. Dad lay stretched out across the whole room. She placed Ninen on his chest and the animal moved around cautiously there, curiously investigating where he had ended up this time.

'See anything special?' Harriet asked.

Dad lifted up the rabbit, inspected him, looked underneath.

'I don't see anything,' said Dad.

'Look at the tag.'

He sat up, perched his glasses lower, and there was the

wooden tag with Harriet's name, and he turned it around to see that Harriet had written 'Dad' on the other side.

'Ninen isn't mine,' Harriet said. 'He's ours.'

At that, Dad closed his eyes, turned away, and pinched the bridge of his nose. It was her and Dad then.

It's windier outside the train window now, the trees that line the tracks are crazy, they seem to be wrestling each other. She looks down at her legs in their black tights. She looks at her dad's feet. He's taken off his boots, is wearing thick woollen socks even though it's the middle of summer. She looks down at her hands, she doesn't like her ugly fingers, doesn't want to look at them. She painted her thumbnail with a marker a few days ago, because she wanted to see what it would look like with nail polish on, but Dad told her to wash it off and now there's just a streak of grey left. Dad's hands on the table. Tanned as though he'd lived a long life outdoors. His hands are right there, just across the table, so close to her, but they feel far away. Untouchable now, after what happened.

They'd had Ninen for a few months. One afternoon she was sitting in her room and waiting for Dad to come home. She was drawing, using markers that were in various stages of drying out. She was making a house and a sun and high clouds, and everything was smiling. A smile on the sun, each cloud got a smiling mouth and narrowed black eyes gazing down at the house, and the house's windows became eyes. She got up to get a fresh marker. The can of them was way up high on the bookcase, and she had to stretch to reach them, and maybe she sensed something just under her heel as she stood on tiptoe, a brush of something soft, the warmth of a body suddenly below her foot. She didn't have time to think, just lowered her heel once she had the can, and the rabbit was caught under it. Harriet threw herself to the floor and picked Ninen up and laid him in her lap, noticed things although she didn't want to, how Ninen's eyes were no longer where they should be. She held him and felt his tentative breaths, felt his heart beating through his soft fur, and she petted him, and she said, 'Please, please, please,' to herself, and again, 'Please, please, please,' and outside the first snow began to fall, the same huge, surreal flakes as always in a first snow, and it got dark fast, the streetlights flickering to life on the street outside, and she held him and felt his heart beat faster, until it beat slower and then stopped. The snow was sticking on the railing of the balcony outside. She squeezed her eyes tight, bent over her rabbit, holding him and gently moving her hand back and forth across his fur, and the afternoon passed slowly but she knew it would end and soon her father would come home and then she would be held accountable for what she'd done.

When Dad arrived he came in with the cold, a gust from the stairwell making its way all the way into her room, and she heard his steps, the rubber soles of his boots squeaking against the floor as he approached, and the clatter of the rolls of film in his pockets, and he opened the door and their eyes met. A few seconds of silence.

'What happened?' Dad asked.

She couldn't respond, nor did she need to, because now he saw the rabbit in her arms. 'What have you done?' he cried, kneeling in front of her, and he noticed the rabbit's head right away and let out a screech and turned away, gazed out of the window, out at the snow that had just fallen on the window-sill, and he seemed to collect himself, and then he screeched again, out of nowhere, and laid a hand on the rabbit's head, and then he bent over and gently buried his face in the dead animal. Harriet could feel the winter chill on Dad's clothes, she saw the back of his head, the thinning hair.

Dad took the rabbit and left, she didn't know where he went. They didn't say a word about Ninen in the coming days. A week passed, and it was like the rabbit had never existed. One day the cage was gone as well. And a few days later she saw the urn in the hall, on the table next to the phone. And it was simply there, like a reminder of what she had done, and each time she walked by it she closed her eyes. At last she assumed that Dad had decided to leave it there, that this was how they would remember him. Spring came, and then summer. And last night, Dad said it was time to bury Ninen. 'You don't have to go to school tomorrow,' he said. 'We're going on a train ride.'

They're sitting on the sunny side of the train, the tabletop is warm. They're approaching another city, and the train slows down. Harriet watches a plastic bag from Domus do quick somersaults down a street and disappear. The well-pruned hedges shake in the breeze, irritated. The train passes subur-ban streets. She sees people outside their houses, watching the

sad. Just minutes after their wild shouting she would seem unbothered, but Dad remained anxious, pacing back and forth, unable to recover for hours. And after each incident Mom would come to Yana's room and sit on the edge of her bed. Like some sort of damage control. Those moments were always the best, because she would tell Yana she loved her.

Just a week or so before Mom disappeared, Mom and Dad were going to a friend's for dinner and Yana came along, as she always did. They sat her on a sofa, gave her a bowl of candy, and put a movie on the TV. The strange scents of an unfamiliar home, the conversations from the kitchen sounding tinny and warped against the tile walls. When the movie was over she wasn't brave enough to ask them to put on a new one, and she waited to go home until at last she fell asleep, and she woke up when Mom shook her gently and picked her up, and all the lights were sharp, people she didn't know patted her head, thick voices said: 'She's awfully tired now.' A chill as the front door opened, and in the taxi she lay against her mother's breast and saw the traffic lights and streetlights pass through rain-splashed windows. She remembers all of it, her parents' hoarse whispers as they walked through the night together, the bitching about the couple they'd just dined and laughed with, Dad's anger when the taxi driver went the wrong way. Then Mom carried her all the way up to the apartment, and the instant they opened the door they heard the familiar scrape of paws on the parquet as Loser darted over from the living room, and Mom and Dad fell to their knees and let the little creature overpower them. He jumped up at Mom, then Dad, then Mom again.

'He's taking turns saying hi,' Dad said in delight. 'He's so democratic.'

Mom made a noise that sounded like a muffled scream. She took a few steps away. 'I can't take it any more,' she called to the apartment.

'What's wrong now?' Dad said.

'Every time we come home – every time.'

'What?'

'Every time, you say Loser is democratic. How many times can a person say that? I'm going to lose my mind.'

Mom went to the bathroom, closed the door, and locked it. Dad was still standing in the hall, and Yana could see the humiliation and the rage grappling inside him. Then he leaped into action. Quick steps to the bathroom; he tugged at the door. 'Open up!' he shouted. He pounded and pounded at it and now Yana knew this was the start of something that would end poorly. He banged at the door so hard that Loser was frightened and ran off, and at last Mom unlocked the door.

'How can it bother you so much for me to say that?' he shouted. 'How can it be so fucking terrible for you?'

And they were off. Yana hurried to the small guest bath-room, brushed her teeth and filled the sink, and when she washed her hands with soap the water looked like milk. Outside, her parents' argument ramped up and took on a life of its own; it wasn't about Loser any more, he was just a meaningless catalyst for something bigger, and the apartment rattled with their voices; she went into her room and lay down on her bed, listening to the sounds. Often, when her parents fought, she would imagine that what she heard out there were cries for help from some people who were trapped, a man and a woman who were locked up somewhere but desperately wanted to get out. And later, when they were quiet, she imagined that they had given up, that they understood no one was coming to rescue them. She had turned on all the lights in her room because she didn't like long shadows on the floor, and she lay gazing at the ceiling. The shouts became fewer and further between until at last they were silent, and she heard them moving around in different rooms. There was a knock on the door, and there stood Mom. She sat down on the edge of the bed but said nothing, just sat there smiling at Yana, brushing away a few strands of hair that had fallen over her forehead.

'Are you still mad at each other?' Yana asked.

'A little.' Mom ran her hand across the bedspread. 'Does it make you upset when we fight?'

'I don't know,' Yana replied. 'A little.'

'I feel so bad that you have to listen to all that.'

Headlights made their way through a gap in the curtains, illuminating the room like silver spears slowly slicing through the ceiling before vanishing.

'Have you ever been in love?' Mom asked.

'I don't know,' said Yana.

'You don't know?' she asked. 'Have you ever felt butterflies in your stomach when you thought about a boy?'

'I don't know,' she said. 'I don't think I want to say.'

'But you can tell me, sweetie. I'm your mother. I won't tell anyone else, I promise.'

Yana hesitated.

'I won't tell a soul,' Mom said. 'Now tell me.'

'There's a boy in my class who I think about sometimes.'

'What do you think about?'

'I imagine we're lying next to each other in a bed.'

'That's nice,' said Mom. 'What else?'

'That's all. We just lie there.'

'That's wonderful. That's how love should be, when you're little.' She smiled, and it made her look almost sad. 'Good. You think about lying next to someone, and that's all there is to it. When you get older, it will be different. I'm not saying it will be worse, but it will seem bigger and more serious somehow. There's a weight over everything. And sometimes I don't know what to do with all that seriousness. I want to be like you sometimes, and just dream about lying next to a boy.'

Mom lay down in bed next to her, and they both looked up at the ceiling.

'One time when I was little, we visited a family to buy their rabbit,' Mom said. 'And there was a boy there, a few years older than me. It was his rabbit, and I guess he was tired of it. He just stayed on his bed, reading a comic book. We hardly spoke. But, still. I couldn't stop thinking about him afterwards. I can still picture what he looked like.'

'Did you fall in love with him?' Yana asked.

'No, not in love, really. But maybe I would have liked to lie next to him in a bed.'

Yana laughed. All of a sudden she felt her forehead go cold, because she had told, but her chest go warm, because she had shared a big secret with Mom. She knew her parents' fight wasn't over, it might pick up again soon, but it was as if Mom had paused to catch her breath there on Yana's bed, because she stayed put, made no move to get up. Yana had her now, for a little while, and she didn't want to move out of fear that something would be interrupted, that Mom would think of something else and get up and leave.

'What are you going to be when you grow up?' Mom asked.

'I don't know,' Yana replied. 'A chef, maybe.'

'Good,' said Mom. 'Then I'll come to your restaurant. Every time I do, I'll complain about the food and demand to speak to the chef.' Mom ducked her head down to Yana's belly, rubbed her nose against her navel, and Yana grabbed Mom's ears. When Mom looked up again, she looked like she'd just woken up, her hair on end. Then she dipped her head down again, and it tickled so much Yana howled and tried to wiggle free. Mom sat up in bed and whispered, 'Time for you and me to sneak out of here and go get some ice cream.'

'But I already brushed my teeth.'

'Don't worry about that,' said Mom.

A surreal feeling as they got out of bed. Were they going out in the middle of the night? Mom brought her index finger to her lips, and they sneaked into the hall and put on their shoes. When they opened the front door to leave,

Dad appeared in the doorway to the kitchen. 'Where are you going?'

'We're going out for a bit,' Mom said tersely.

'It's eleven-thirty,' Dad said. 'It's too late to go out with her.'

Mom nudged Yana into the stairwell and slammed the door, and she laughed in delight and Yana's heart was pounding under her jacket, happy and afraid all at the same time. The elevator, which only sometimes sounded strange, was clattering worse than ever right now, as though it wanted to raise objections as well: even the elevator thought it was too late, and on the way down the ceiling light made Mom's eyes black and she looked worried. Was she already regretting this?

It was night, but the city was bustling. Teenagers hung around aimlessly outside bars that had just closed. They passed a gang of guys kicking at each other; Yana didn't know if they were fooling around or if it was serious. Mom held her hand all the while, her palm warm and damp. 'That's where we're going,' she said, pointing at a McDonald's sign far down the street, and Yana slowed down.

'Dad says I'm not allowed to eat there.'

'That's nonsense,' Mom said. 'That's no way to live.'

She felt anxious as they went inside, the memories of all the times Dad had pointed at McDonald's locations as they passed by and said, 'That's where you get fat.'

They walked into the late-night commotion, Mom perfectly at home in the chaos, as though she'd seen all this a thousand times before and it couldn't shock her in the least. Mom ordered the largest sundae with extra caramel sauce and got one for herself too, and they sat down at a window table where they could look at everything going on outside, just a thin pane of glass between them and the Stockholm night.

Yana ate her ice cream slowly. Mom had taken a few straws from the cash register and for a while all her focus was on tying them together. She didn't want to say what she was doing, just that it was a present. After some time she was finished, and she placed the necklace over Yana's head. She decided she should make one for herself, so they could be the same, so everyone could see they belonged together. With great concentration, she tied together another necklace of straws.

'Do you remember your grandfather, my dad?' she asked. 'You were pretty little when he died.'

'I remember him. He had glasses that made his eyes look small.'

'That's right.'

'He gave me a feather once.'

'Yes, an eagle feather, which he told lots of stories about.'

'He was nice.'

'He tried. But sometimes it was like he only had eyes for those eagles, and he forgot to look at me. I remember when he turned sixty and I brought him a cake, and for once we started to have a real conversation, and I asked him what he thought the most important thing in life was. And you know what he said? Freedom. And it made me sad to hear him say that, because I thought he would say that the most important thing in life was me.'

Mom stopped talking and fast-food-restaurant sounds took over: a machine rattling out crushed ice, the tentative rumble of the coolers. Yana looked down at her hands. Someone had spilled salt, and it showed up clearly against the red tabletop, and a few soft French fries had been left by the customer who'd sat here right before them.

'Do you know what the most important thing in my life is?' Mom asked.

'No.'

Mom looked at her with a smile, and now Yana was smiling too. 'Guess,' said Mom.

'Me?'

'Yes!' Mom threw her hands in the air and made fists, a gesture of victory. Then she reached one hand across the table, and Yana took it. 'No matter what, I will never leave you,' Mom said. 'It will be you and me for ever.'

Yana looks at her watch; it's as though time is shrinking the closer she gets to the station. Sweden passes by outside the train window: she sees gleaming lakes, and when a breeze blows over them it looks like they're cold, like they've got goosebumps. Why didn't she ever travel? She's spent her whole life living at home in her apartment; everything she has missed is passing outside the window. This wasn't how her life was supposed to turn out; this isn't what she pictured that night in McDonald's when her mom promised never to leave her. She remembers the cold ice cream burning into her brain, and Mom crying out when it was gone: 'Let's buy another one!'

'No, I don't want more,' Yana said.

'Yes, one more!' Mom got up to go to the counter.

'I don't feel like more ice cream, Mom.'

Mom sat back down, and she received a text alert and searched through her coat pockets for her phone. Her face was illuminated by the screen. She smiled, fired off a quick response, and waited for a reaction, which arrived, and she started typing again. Mom put down the phone after a while, stuck it back in her coat.

'Who was that?' Yana asked.

'Dad.'

'What did he say?'

'Awfully sweet things,' she said. 'He wants us to be friends again.'

And they got up and walked hand-in-hand through the night, back down the sparkling street. When they arrived home, Dad had turned out the lights; there was just a yellow glow from the kitchen, he'd lit a candle there and on the table was a charcuterie board. Mom followed Yana into her room and tucked her in. 'I'll do it nice and tight like a mummy,' Mom said, folding the covers under Yana so the shape of her was visible on the bed. 'What is the most important thing in my life?' Mom asked.

'Me,' Yana answered.

Mom did her victory gesture again, two fists in the air. She turned the lights off on her way out, one by one, and then she was gone and Yana lay in the dark, listening to a wine bottle opening and low conversation from the kitchen. She could smell smoke – Mom was having a cigarette. And they talked together and she couldn't make out what they were saying, but she could tell that it was kind and warm. They were friends again. Suddenly the low voices got even quieter, falling into unclear murmurs. Something sparked her curiosity, a giggle and a lengthy silence. She got out of bed and gently opened the door to her bedroom. Quiet as a mouse, she went out to the dark hall.

'And who was it?' she heard Dad whisper. Someone refilled their wine. The familiar sound of Dad rotating the liquid in his glass a few times, and the foot of the glass scraping on the table. 'Who was she lying next to?' Dad asked.

'I don't know,' Mom replied. 'She just said it was a boy in her class.'

Chapter 10

Oskar

The irritation begins as a vague ripple in his stomach. He tries again and again to connect his cell phone to the internet by way of the 2G network, but it just churns and churns and the site keeps going down, not once since they left Stockholm has he managed to connect. He's alone, a prisoner on this train, totally under her control now. He doesn't want to be there, he wants to go home, and so the train's movement in the wrong direction is an ongoing provocation, and he knows very well where it will end; he knows himself well enough these days, recognises the signs. Soon he'll crack and say something that will only make it worse.

He saw a therapist for a few weeks; she had a head full of exercises she wanted him to try when he was about to blow up. A thought exercise she suggested for when the darkness came over him: he should imagine walking along a poorly maintained gravel path in the summer after a downpour. The path is filled with deep puddles he must get past. And when a puddle pops up in front of him, he should stop and think, 'Oops, there's a puddle.' And then decide to walk around it.

The therapist had asked Oskar to name a place where he feels perfectly calm, where nothing can bother him, and his immediate reply was the Stockholm archipelago. Driving in his car down the narrow, paved roads, the sea moving in and out of sight on either side. He could do that for hours. Once he finished training to be an estate agent, he applied to work at a small firm that offered houses in the archipelago. He got the job, and ever since that was how he spent his days, out in his car, heavy keyrings in his coat pocket and a bundle of prospectuses on the passenger seat. He showed the houses as though they were his own. He knew he would never be able to afford a summer home there, but nor did he need to. Showing those houses was enough, and at least once a day, often once he was far out in the islands, far away from the built-up areas, he would be walking through a forest on his way to a place with a view of the sea, and a realisation would come to him with a crazy, almost desperate power: he felt he belonged there. That he was meant to be there. The deep blue water, the sun-bleached docks, the dry evergreen forest; it was so familiar on an almost instinctive level that he felt he must have lived there in another life. He felt gentle out on those islands, and each time he returned home at night the spell was broken; his safety catch released once more.

The first step is to recognise the things that risk launching him into fury. Right now it's not hard to name them.

126

He's on his way to a place he doesn't want to visit. And the woman who's making him go there won't even tell him why. Something happened on a trip Harriet took here with her father, Bo, something so important that she's now forcing him to come along.

Of course Bo is involved. Always Bo. Harriet never wanted to say a word about her mother, but she could linger on Bo for hours. To think that this man, who was so absent from Harriet's life, could still affect her so much. They hardly ever see him, but he's always there anyway, an anxious gleam in her eyes when the topic of him comes up.

During Oskar's first years with Harriet he didn't meet Bo a single time; he wasn't part of her life. He got to know her father through the stories she told. Oskar's first encounter with Bo took place in their stairwell. It was a Sunday, and Yana was a newborn. Oskar was heading down to the basement to use the tenant association's grubby little sauna. Someone had put up a sign that read SPA on the door to the sauna area. Once he had brought a marker down with him and put quotation marks around the word 'SPA' and it always improved his mood to see his correction. Oskar was wearing a robe that day, and he darted out of the apartment so quickly that he almost crashed directly into Bo. He knew at once this must be Harriet's father. The big camera bags, the small eyes, which he recognised from a photograph on the bookcase, Bo and Harriet at a fast-food place. Had he been standing there long? Why hadn't he rung the doorbell? He called for Harriet, who came hurrying over, all wound up and out of sorts.

'What are you doing here?' she asked.

'I had a shoot a few blocks away,' Bo said. 'I finished early and thought I would come up and say hi.'

'Oskar was just heading down to the sauna,' she said. 'Maybe you'd like to join him?'

'I can skip the sauna,' Oskar said.

'No,' Harriet said. 'Dad loves the sauna, don't you, Dad?'

'Sauna?' said Bo. He grimaced as he picked up the camera bags and carried them into the apartment.

The suggestion had made Oskar go cold, and he didn't understand what Harriet was up to; it would take several years for him to realise that there was nothing odd about it, because this was always her greatest goal, to get Bo to like Oskar and to get Oskar to like Bo.

'Sure, I could sauna,' said Bo.

Oskar and Bo walked in silence down the stairs to the basement, door after door that must be carefully unlocked, so many unnecessary locks to protect all the crap behind the bars. 'I'm the one who put those quotation marks there,' Oskar said as they came to the door. Bo looked at the sign, and then they went in. They took off their clothes and sat on the top bench. 'What kind of shoot were you at?' Oskar asked.

'It was for a dog food ad,' Bo said, pouring a scoopful of water on the rocks, and Oskar was struck by the easy way he had taken over their sauna time, as though this were his sauna and Oskar were the guest. 'There were three dogs to photograph, and when I got to the studio I could hear them barking, they were closed in a room. I asked what was wrong, and they said they'd let the dogs go two days without food.'

'Why?' Oskar asked.

'So they would throw themselves at the food when we were shooting, so that when you saw the pictures you would understand how good it must be.'

'Shit.'

'Then I saw how they were holding the dogs still and putting some sort of syrup on their muzzles. The dogs went crazy, trying to get rid of the syrup, they were licking their lips in a panic, and the team did all that to the dogs because when a dog licks its lips it appears to be enjoying its food.'

'Disgusting,' said Oskar.

'I just packed up my stuff and left. I don't work with people like that.'

Oskar shot a cautious glance in Bo's direction; the old man had closed his eyes in the heat, was leaning back against the wooden wall, relaxed but ready, sinewy, explosive. A large tattoo of an eagle on his arm: it must have been done a long time ago and was now spreading through his skin. His body was totally hairless except for around his genitals, where he looked aggressive and dangerous, his penis fortified by steel wool. He had started sweating immediately, and his whole body gleamed and glittered in the weak yellow light.

So there he sat, the man Oskar had only heard spoken of on occasion, in vague fragments of memories from Harriet's childhood. There was something fractured about how he spoke, a trait he recalled from the time in the bar on

Vasagatan when Harriet had called him up to say she loved him. It was like the reverse of a cracking voice, where something bright and shrill broke through the darkness now and then. But Bo wasn't much of a talker. He sat there quietly, eyes closed. At some point he bent forward for a while, and when he sat back up again the metal cross he wore around his neck touched his chest and he gave a cry. But he simply kept sitting there, didn't take off the cross, didn't make any attempt to avoid the pain.

When they got back to the apartment, Harriet brought over Yana, who was sleeping in her stroller, and Bo looked down and smiled. 'Beautiful,' he said, as he took off his jacket.

'She'll probably wake up soon,' said Harriet. 'Then you can hold her.'

She served him a glass of wine, which he never touched. Oskar prepared dinner, chicken in a red-wine sauce, even as he observed Bo walking around the apartment. His movements were slow, but always exact, as though he were always conserving energy, gathering up his strength for some great effort. His boots were large but didn't make a sound. Oskar kept having to look up from the sauce to see where Bo had gone. Suddenly he was at the bookcase, reading the titles.

'Dad!' Harriet called. 'Can't you help Oskar with the sauce?'

'I don't need any help with the sauce,' said Oskar.

'But you never get it quite right. And Dad's red-wine sauce is just the best.'

And Bo was there, peering into the saucepan. He took a

ladle and gently stirred the reduction. Tasted it. 'Do you have more stock?' he asked. Oskar fetched it from the fridge and handed it over. Bo looked at the bottle and smiled. He put it down. 'You have to use real stock.' He stared down at the sauce, stirring it slowly. Went to the spice rack and ran his fingers along the jars.

'What are you looking for?' Oskar asked.

He didn't respond, but found the thyme and returned to the pan. The sauce belonged to Bo now, and Oskar was a spectator.

Dinner was eaten in silence, and Oskar felt a tenderness for Harriet as he watched her across the table, bent over her food and wound tight as a fiddle string. She wiped her mouth with a napkin now and then, always with a slight smile on her lips. It was like coming in at the tail end of a very long and wrenching film, the few lines of dialogue loaded with incomprehensibility. Bo didn't seem bothered by the silence in the least, he just sat there in the gentle clatter of silverware, among throat-clearings and mumbles about passing the salt, and when he had finished his chicken he took another helping of sauce and poured it over his plate.

'I saw Amelia the other day,' said Harriet.

'You did?' Bo's fork froze mid-bite. 'Where did you see her?'

'At the pool, or . . . yes, it was her.'

Bo put down his silverware. 'What do you mean?' he asked.

'I was swimming at the pool, and when I was showering afterwards the woman next to me was missing a nipple.'

'Did you talk to her?'

'I didn't have time. I was so surprised. She went to the changing room without seeing me.'

'But it was her?'

'It looked just as I had imagined.'

Bo picked up his silverware again, put a potato on his plate, and pressed his fork through it. 'That doesn't mean it was her.'

'No, but I recognised her.'

'She doesn't even live in Stockholm,' he said.

'Dad!' Harriet cried. 'It was Amelia. I recognise my own sister.' And her eyes got shiny and she crooked her neck down over the table so her black hair made a curtain around her. She buried her face in her hands.

'Bitty,' said Dad.

'Bitty,' said Harriet.

To Oskar, this sister Amelia remained a mystery. Harriet talked about her sometimes: early memories from their childhood together, before the divorce. But what happened after that he never found out; he only knew that they had been split up in the divorce and later on they lost contact entirely. Harriet didn't want to talk about Amelia, or about why they still weren't in touch. And not once had he ever heard her mention her mother's name, except for that one time, at the very beginning, in that bar. The time she said she was a monster.

After dinner they moved over to the little sofa that stood before the fireplace. Bo took some logs from the basket and arranged them for a fire. Oskar offered to fetch some newspaper for kindling. No, that wouldn't be necessary, Bo could light it without any paper. When the fire flared up it sent tiny, glowing sparks out of the fireplace, and Bo watched them carefully, not taking his eyes off them until they were extinguished on the stone hearth. 'Spruce,' said Bo. 'Spruce logs are no good for a fire.' And they drank coffee, and the night was long. Oskar curiously observed the power Bo had over Harriet. It was an energy he'd never encountered before, the ability to have such a negative impact on those around you. And the silence was still oppressive; long stretches of nothing passed as they gazed at the fire, which was fading now, becoming a red glow. Harriet went to the stereo and came back as the first notes of Lou Reed's 'Perfect Day' played, and she sang along to the verse. She picked up a chunk of wood and put it on the coals, then stayed where she was, bent over the fire, her bottom poking out into the room. What was she doing? Then, slowly, she began to sway her ass to the music, and she placed a hand over each cheek. Harriet turned around and looked at her father, and Bo gazed silently at his daughter, and Oskar felt so nervous that he started laughing. Harriet moved closer to her father, a challenge, and Oskar just laughed louder and more shrilly, and the fire launched warning shot after warning shot into the room.

They've often laughed at this incident, and now, sometimes when they're alone, they can find amusement in it, when they recall Bo's reaction in the dim apartment, the fire playing in his glasses and his neutral gaze as he tried to get a handle on the situation. But they've never talked about it for real, just like so many other things in their relationship. She loves to talk about things that have happened to her, she's obsessed with the past, but she wants to select the episodes herself.

The train travels through Sweden. Harriet is slouched in her seat, almost lying down, reading a magazine of the sort that shamelessly runs stories about the Twin Towers' collapse alongside news about Justin Timberlake's relationship with Britney Spears. He takes out his phone, still no service. He plays Snake, but he doesn't have the patience for it, puts down his phone. He looks at his watch; they've been travelling for three hours. 'When will we get there?' he asks.

'I don't know.' She looks up from her magazine. 'There must be another hour to go.'

'An hour?!' He looks down at the table – oops, there's a puddle. He quickly scratches the back of his hand. 'Do you remember the time when Yana was a baby,' he says, 'when you did a porn dance in front of your father?'

She laughs, leans over the table, and looks at him. 'Yeah, I remember that.'

'Why did you do that?'

'What?'

'I was just wondering why you did it.'

She leans back in her seat, her smile slowly vanishing. She inspects her fingernails. 'It shouldn't be that hard to work out,' she says. 'I did it because I wanted him to see me.'

Oskar nods. That was surprisingly honest.

'After Dad went home that evening, I thought it went

pretty well,' she says. 'I didn't break down until later that night. I went to the kitchen and cried. For hours.'

'Why did you cry?'

'Because he didn't look at Yana. Not once all evening did he even glance her way.'

Oskar takes her hand across the table. 'I don't remember any of that. Why didn't you wake me up?'

'You wouldn't have been interested.'

'Why would you say that?'

She lets go of his hand, shrugs.

'I've never met anyone like your dad,' said Oskar. 'His very presence in a room could shut everyone up.'

Harriet starts laughing.

'Why are you laughing?'

'Who are you talking about? You or my dad?'

'What do you mean?' he asks.

She doesn't respond, just looks out of the window.

He leans across the table, towards her. 'Could you explain,' he says, making his tone sharper. 'Could you explain to me what you mean?'

Then she leans his way, coming close, their foreheads almost touching. 'Only once will you catch sight of yourself, and that moment alone will be either the happiest or bitterest moment of your life.'

Oskar gets up and walks off without a word. He stands between two cars, stays there for a while, in the space where nothing muffles the sound and the train is so loud that it almost makes you crazy.

Chapter 11

Harriet

Dad has been gone a long time now. Harriet looks at her watch. She has to blink each time the second hand moves, sixty blinks per minute, and if she misses one she has to start over. Dad gave her the watch because he wants her to learn how to tell the time; he had no way of knowing the kind of problems it would create for her. When the hands point in certain directions it makes a sad mouth, and then it makes her feel sad to look at it. The numbers force their way in; she can't even look at some of them. The ones with eyes or mouths are the worst, like 8 and 9. And all those demands that appear the minute she looks at the watch; she has to count and blink and do different things in a certain order before the second hand has gone all the way around. There are so many things she does that she doesn't want anyone to know about. Like how she needs to think a loving thought about everything she sees before it vanishes. Most of the time it's possible to do this in secret, without anyone seeing, except here on the train where it all goes by so fast, all the houses and signs streaming by: she thinks Dad has already noticed that she's up to something. But it's even harder to hide the things she has to do with her body. If she looks to the right one time she feels bad for the left, so she has to look that way too. If she lifts her left hand twice she must lift her right hand twice. She does it to compensate, so that things are fair between her body parts. Other things she does, she can't explain. Sometimes she has to stand up and spin around a few times, look around carefully, or else she worries that reality will bend and she'll fall through it and tumble out somewhere else. Now she sees Dad coming her way through the car, and she immediately stops doing all of this, hides the watch under her sleeve. He places a plate with a slice of chocolate cake in front of her on the table, along with a can of Loranga. A cup of coffee for himself.

'There was a hell of a line,' Dad says, sinking into his seat. She takes a bite of the cake, sees the marks her teeth leave in the icing. It looks like a rat has been chewing on it, she can't look at it. She opens the Loranga and takes a drink, and she remembers the time her parents called her into the kitchen to tell her they were getting a divorce. They gave her a soda that had been in the pantry, and the bubbles filled the roof of her mouth until she started coughing and some soda came out of her nose, but, even so, Dad wasn't upset. 'There's something we need to tell you,' Mom had said with that peculiar look on her face, which Harriet couldn't make sense of.

'There's something I have to tell you,' Dad says, and Harriet nods and puts the cake down on the paper plate. 'We're on our way to say goodbye to Bitty, and we'll be there soon, but before we get off I thought we could decide to say goodbye to a few more things while we're at it.'

Dad waits for Harriet's reaction. A conductor goes by, and he lets him pass. 'I thought we could say goodbye to secrets.' The sun is in Dad's eyes, and he raises a hand so he can have a look at his daughter. 'Do you understand what I mean?' he says.

'Yes,' Harriet replies.

'We have to start being honest with each other, don't we?'

'Yes.' Harriet picks up the cake, breaking off a piece this time so she doesn't have to look at her disgusting tooth marks in it.

'I thought we could ask each other questions that we have to answer honestly. I'll ask you a question, and then you'll ask me a question. What do you say to that?'

'OK,' she replies.

'Then I'll start.' He drinks his coffee. 'What book are you reading right now?'

Harriet laughs, dares to look Dad in the eye: she can see that he's smiling at her. '*The Children's Bible*,' she answers.

'Right,' Dad says with a laugh. 'OK, good. Now it's your turn.'

Harriet looks down at her cake. 'OK ...' she says, then falls silent. 'What ... book are you reading?'

'I'm not reading a book right now,' Dad replies. 'I can't

read at night any more. It only gets me all worked up and then I can't sleep.'

'I get worked up from reading *The Children's Bible* too,' Harriet says. 'It's kind of scary sometimes.'

Dad had given her the book the other day, and Harriet had read some of it each evening since, and it was like the stories in the book made sounds; each time she opened it she heard the Bible at top volume, sandals on gravel, people screaming, the sound of spears piercing human flesh. And God was always invisible, but ever-present, everywhere, when people did incredible things to avoid his wrath. Abraham, for instance, chained up his son to burn him alive, just to make God happy. The story of a sleazy city God decided to burn down one day, to kill everyone who lived there. Only one family would be spared, because they were good people. When God started burning and murdering, they were ordered to simply leave the city, run for their lives, and God's rule was: they were absolutely not allowed to look back, but the mom couldn't help herself, she wanted to see what God was doing to the city, and the instant she turned around she was frozen into a statue. She died on the spot, and Harriet couldn't understand why. What kind of weird rule was that? God killed her because . . . she turned around? What was her actual crime?

At least Harriet's crime was clear. She had bitten her sister and ruined her body for ever. When she sat with her back against the fence, waiting for Dad to come pick her up that day, she felt some sort of relief, because at least it was obvious.

She had committed a crime and would pay for it. Days and weeks passed and nothing happened, no punishment was meted out. She wanted to call Amelia and apologise, but Dad said that wasn't a good idea. Several times after that she had asked to talk to Amelia, but she was always told no. She soon realised that the silence itself was the punishment. Now it's been a year since it happened, and she still hasn't seen her sister. She hasn't even gotten to talk to her on the phone. Harriet writes about Amelia in her diary almost every day and makes lists of what they would do when they saw each other again. She never thinks up new things, only activities they've done together before, things she wants to do with her again. She ranks the activities from one to five, and at the very top of the list, almost every time, is 'Lie in bed and listen to music Amelia likes'.

Dad cautiously sips his hot coffee, dipping his upper lip in the drink, then sets his cup down again. 'OK, my turn to ask a question,' he says. 'Sometimes when I come into your room, I notice you hiding a photo under your pillow. What's in that photo?'

'It's . . .' Her heart was pounding. She didn't know Dad had discovered she had the photo. And she was afraid to lie, because what if Dad knew more than he was letting on? 'It's a picture of you and me,' she replies.

She had found it on Dad's desk, a black and white picture of her and Dad at McDonald's. They were both wearing necklaces made of straws Mom had tied together, and they were hugging each other and laughing at something; she doesn't remember what was so funny. Harriet used it as a bookmark for her current book, and each night, before she turned out the light, she lay in bed looking at the picture. The photo was glossy, and it was like the memory became more golden as it gleamed in the light of her bedside lamp. She couldn't get enough of it, couldn't stop looking at it.

'Why do you hide it?' Dad asks.

'I don't know,' Harriet says.

'Did you think I would be mad?'

'I don't know.'

Dad takes off his glasses and presses his thumb and index finger to his temples, slowly massaging the sides of his head with his long fingers. 'You know, don't you, that you can look at that picture as much as you want? You don't need to hide it.'

'Yeah,' she says.

'OK,' says Dad. 'Your turn again.'

'But I don't have any questions, Dad.'

'Of course you do. You can ask me anything.'

Her chocolate cake is too warm now, the sun has been shining on the table and the chocolate has melted and pooled on the white plate. She wants to dip a finger in it and lick it, but she resists the urge. 'Why don't you want me to see Amelia?' She knows it's a dangerous question, but now it's asked.

'That's not it,' Dad says. 'I do want you to see each other. I want to see Amelia too.'

'So Mom doesn't want us to?'

'When we got divorced, we fought a lot. And one day she called to say that she would just be Amelia's mom, and I would just be your dad.'

'Why?'

'I don't know. But I've always thought it was wrong. No one has the right to separate two siblings, or parents from children. And I've tried to fight it. But now a lawyer has decided that's how it's going to be.'

'Decided what?'

'Well . . . ' Dad said. 'That you two would be split up.'

'So Mom isn't my mom any more?'

'She'll always be your mom.'

In the days following the divorce, Mom had called Harriet now and then to ask how she was doing. But after the fight with Amelia on the dock, she hadn't called even once. Harriet realised that her only chance of being in touch with her sister was to be stealthy about it. On one of those long afternoons when Dad was off working she went into his bedroom. On his desk she found a padded envelope with Mom's name on it. She saw that it contained bills addressed to her. She sat down at Dad's desk and wrote to her sister. It ended up being a long letter in which she told her sister all the things that she'd been thinking about during the year in which they'd had no contact. She ended the letter by writing: 'Sorry.' And then she wrote it one more time, in bigger letters and enclosed by a heart in red marker: 'SORRY.' Then, from her diary, she tore all the pages of lists she'd made of things she wanted to do with Amelia. Scraps of paper filled with her dreams, stuffed into the envelope alongside the letter. She licked and sealed it and hoped Dad wouldn't notice it had gotten fatter. The next day, the envelope was missing from Dad's desk, and her wait began. The reaction from the other side of the country had come the day before yesterday. Harriet was lying in bed, reading *The Children's Bible*, and heard the phone ring in the hall, and it was unusual for it to ring at all, at their house, and especially not so late. She heard Dad pick up, and answer as he always did by slowly reciting their phone number. After this he didn't participate much in the conversation, just low *hmm*s followed by protracted silence. He hung up, and soon he was standing in the doorway. She could tell he was angry: he was breathing through his nose, his eyes even smaller, tiny and dark like a crustacean's, but still he used the same quiet voice. 'What have you done?' he said. 'I told you not to contact your sister.'

'I didn't.'

'You're lying to me. Mom called and told me you wrote a letter to Amelia and smuggled it into the envelope of bills. You have to realise that she doesn't want to talk to you.'

Dad left. And Harriet stayed put, lying on her bed. She looked at Amelia's empty bed across the room. A book her sister had once been reading was still on the nightstand. It was open, spine up, as though she had only stepped out for a moment to use the bathroom. Harriet observed the small grease spots on the wall above her sister's bed, traces of the putty she'd used to put up posters of her idols, artistes Harriet had never heard of. The noises Dad made getting ready for bed. And as she lay there she felt anxious in a new and heavy way, and she couldn't figure out why. She was worried about something her thoughts hadn't quite grasped yet, and she knew if she just fought her brain a little she would untangle it, but it didn't happen: she never figured out what it was.

The train enters a curve and objects on the table begin to move. Dad doesn't notice that one of his lenses is about to roll onto the floor, and Harriet thrusts out a hand to catch it, but Dad gets there first, catches it as it falls. He takes out the camera bag, places the heavy lens in its black compartment; she thinks it's satisfying to observe how the lens fits perfectly, made to be there, how it gently settles into its nylon home.

'My turn,' Dad says. 'I've noticed that you pull your hair. Sometimes I see tufts of hair left behind on your pillow. Why do you do that?'

'I don't know,' says Harriet. 'It hurts, but it also feels good.'

'Oh, sweetie . . .'

She looks up at her father, who grimaces and looks out of the window.

'You shouldn't hurt yourself, OK?'

Harriet nods.

'What makes you do it? Are you sad?'

She can't respond, gazes down at the half-eaten treat before her.

'Are you sad about what happened with Amelia?'

'I feel sad every time I think about Amelia,' she replies. 'I want to tell her I'm sorry for what happened on the dock.'

'What did happen?'

Harriet doesn't respond. Would she be able to tell him, even if she wanted to? It's been a year since it happened, her memories have grown fuzzy and parts of it keep falling away. There are some things she can still recount exactly. When she bit Amelia and when her skin was ripped away from her body, it sounded like when someone pulls the halves of a wet rag apart.

'What did Amelia say to you?' Dad asks. 'What happened on that dock? Why were you so angry?'

Harriet looks down, closes her fingers around a lock of hair; beneath her eyelids it stings and strains, she presses her lips together hard. 'I don't remember, Dad.' She meets her father's eyes and doesn't look away this time, because she knows how her life is going to be and she has to be strong. She is a girl on the run, and she must always be in motion, can't think about things that have happened. She must never look back, or she will be turned to stone.

Chapter 12

Yana

The first time she flew in an aeroplane was on a high-school class trip to Gotland. The plane was small, only forty seats, everyone boarded with their heads ducked and found their spots. A flight attendant approached just before they took off: would Yana be willing to change seats, sit a little closer to the front of the plane? It had to do with the weight and balance of the plane, and she rose quickly, embarrassed. She didn't want to fly after that. Trains are so nice, because there is so much more space; there's room for her here. She sits at her window seat and stretches her legs. The train is approaching her station and she should start gathering her belongings now, but she's interested in something about the photo album she hadn't considered before. On one page is a picture of Mom as a little girl, sitting on the bench at Malma Station. Above her hangs a sign that reads 'MALMA STATION'. She has buried her face in her hands. Under the photo is a white area, it's clear that there used to be another picture there. Why did someone take it out? She runs her fingertips across the white area. There's so much she'll never know. This story has so many blind spots. Yana looks at the picture and tries to find her mother in it, but when she looks at it she sees only herself. She was like that, that worried expression in her eyes, always afraid that something was about to fall apart, or that something already had.

On Sundays, Dad was always out doing showings in the archipelago from morning until late in the evening, and Mom didn't work because the library was closed, so it became their special day. Each Sunday Mom and Yana went swimming together. Yana liked everything about it, except the swimming itself. She was ashamed of being fat and thought everyone was staring at her when she walked around in her bathing suit. But everything before and after this was Yana's favourite: being alone with her mother, walking to the subway with her, sitting with her by the entrance afterwards and eating a chocolate oat-ball. Sundays with Mom were simple and wonderful. But this time was different. She sensed it immediately. Mom wasn't acting like her usual self: she was in a hurry to change, took Yana by the hand and rushed her into the pool area. There Mom ran into some man, and they sat by the edge of the pool to chat and Yana had to swim alone. Mom showed no interest in her at all, only waving now and then when she caught sight of her in the water. Yana didn't understand why they were whispering, sitting so close, shoulder to shoulder. She tried to swim up to them to find out what they were talking about, but it was too loud in the pool. The lifeguard was making excessive use of his whistle: each time a rule was broken he pointed with one hand and blew it hard and the shriek of it bounced off the tile walls and sliced through her brain.

In the shower afterwards she asked who Mom had been talking to. 'A friend,' Mom replied. 'I thought he could join us for our snack.'

Yana didn't respond as she dried herself roughly with the towel.

'If it's OK with you?' Mom said.

'Yeah,' Yana replied quietly.

Soon they were standing in line at the cafeteria, she and Mom and the man. She didn't dare to look at him, noticed his suit trousers, a white shirt neatly tucked in, and a shiny belt. It was his treat, he said, and he took a wallet from his back pocket. 'What do you usually get?' he asked.

'I usually get to pick, either soda or a chocolate oat-ball,' said Yana. 'And usually I pick a chocolate oat-ball.'

'Know what?' said the man. 'Today you can have both.'

They sat by the glass windows and she gazed out at the parking lot. He asked her questions, where she went to school and what her favourite classes were, and at first she gave brief answers, but as time went on she offered more details. After a while she was brave enough to look up at him and meet his gaze. He had a kind voice, and when he asked a question he listened carefully to her response. He took out his jacket and handed her a little box of beads. It was a present, he said. How did he know she loved beads?

149

'Maybe you'd like to make a bracelet for your mom?' he said.

Yana looked at Mom, who had a strange smile on. She opened the box and he helped her tie a knot at one end of a string so she could start. He kept asking questions, sifting through the beads and suggesting different colours for the bracelet, but he was clueless, had no idea what Mom liked. Mom's favourite colour was blue, and Yana's favourite colour was pink, so she picked out only pink and blue beads and threaded them alternately on the string, and outside the towering clouds sailed swiftly across the sky, the sun shining and hiding by turns as she concentrated on the string. When she was finished, she handed the bracelet to Mom, who said, 'Ooh,' and put it on. Yana picked up another string. 'I'll make one for you now,' she said to the man. 'What's your favourite colour?'

'Brown,' said the man.

She poked through the beads. 'Which kind of brown?' she asked. 'There are lots.'

'Like your mother's eyes.'

Yana looked up at her mother, who leaned across the table and looked at her and made big eyes and looked funny, and Yana laughed and sorted the beads, happy in that moment, unhappy in that moment, butterflies in her stomach, dread beating on her from inside, thumping against her ribs. She picked out the darkest brown beads, lined them up on the table.

'Didn't they have some candy over there too?' the man said. 'Run along and buy yourself a treat.'

'May I?' she asked.

'Get whatever you want.'

He gave her some money and she ran over to the little kiosk, peered into the display, four white plastic tubs with raspberry boats and vanilla squares, and small silver tongs resting in one of them. From her place in line she couldn't see the table where Mom was sitting with the man, and she just wanted to make sure they were still there, that everything was all right, so she veered out of line and took a few steps back, and between the café patrons she saw them kissing. Yana was frozen on the spot for a few seconds, just staring at them and their kiss, and then she quickly turned around and dashed into the bathroom. She locked the door and sat down on the toilet seat. And she kept sitting there until she heard Mom calling anxiously outside, and knocking at the door. When she came out, the man was gone and they went home. That evening, Mom acted as though nothing had happened: she sat at the kitchen table having a glass of wine while Dad made dinner.

That night, Yana couldn't sleep. She lay in bed, and through the wide-open window she heard the melancholy sounds of the night outside, someone recycling empty bottles on the square, bottles dropped in one by one to be crushed in a sea of glass. A moped speeding by. And the days that followed were the same, Mom acting like nothing was the matter, like nothing had happened. Yana spent most of her time in her room. Once Dad knocked on her door when she was crying in the window seat. He lingered in the doorway, gazing at her awkwardly. 'Are you OK?' he said after a while.

'Yeah,' she said.

'Were you crying?'

'No.'

He stayed where he was, his gaze vacant. There was no point in talking to him. Their conversations always sounded distorted; conversations with him felt like talking to someone under water. But as he stood there in the doorway, looking at her until he closed the door, she felt sorry for him for the first time, and that gaze she had always felt wary of, it no longer frightened her. He was her father, and there was something he needed to know.

The days that followed were awful yet reminiscent of ordinary ones, and she waited for Mom to come to her and explain what had happened. But time went on. It was so quiet in the apartment, and the closer it got to the weekend the more anxious Yana felt. Saturday night was the longest. On Sunday morning, Mom went out for a run. Dad was standing at the kitchen table, sorting his folders; he would soon head out to show houses. Yana sat at the kitchen table, she knew she and Mom would go swimming again in a while. But she didn't want to go back to the pool. She sat in the kitchen and, her eyes on the tabletop, she began to cry.

'Honey, are you crying?' Dad said. 'Is something wrong?'

And she told him everything. Incoherently, between sobs, she told him what she had seen. Dad said nothing and listened. He held his hand over her back, waited for her tears to stop, occasionally asking a cautious question, wanting more information. 'Have you seen this man before, with Mom?

152

Did he mention his name? Could you have been mistaken?' Or, 'Are you sure they were kissing?'

She tried to answer as best she could, and with every part she told him, her betrayal of Mom grew. 'Mom is going to be so mad at me,' she said.

'She won't be mad,' Dad said. 'You did the right thing, telling me. Now let's wait for Mom to get home, and we'll figure this out.'

Dad seemed calm and collected. He sat down and made some calls, cancelled all his showings, and then he puttered about the kitchen as usual, as if this were just a regular morning. He made hot chocolate for Yana; he'd never done that before. He placed the steaming mug before her and began to clear the dishes. He made a few passes by the window to see if he could spot Mom out on the square. And at last she came home, her face cheerful, as it always was when she had just been for a run. She took her shoes off in the hall.

'You can go to your room now,' Dad said to Yana.

She briefly met Mom's gaze as she passed her in the hall on the way to her bedroom.

'What's going on?' Mom asked. She looked between Dad and Yana.

'Come here,' Dad said. He sat down at the kitchen table.

That was how it went, the time she betrayed her mother.

She stood by her door, listening to their conversation through the crack. This confrontation was different from the usual ones. Typically, the accusations would surge back and forth, and protracted silences would settle over the apartment before it all started up again. This was something different, a slowly rising acceleration: first quiet conversation, where Dad, his voice restrained, demanded to be told what had happened. Mom said at first that she didn't have any idea what Dad was talking about.

'Don't you make me get Yana in here!' he snapped. 'Don't you make me!'

With that, Mom confessed, and after that he launched into what sounded like an interrogation, in which he demanded to know every detail. 'Did you fuck him?' he asked.

'No,' she replied.

He asked again and again, and his voice got tense and strange and then he shouted at the top of his lungs: '*In front of our daughter!*'

Silence.

'You did all of this in front of our daughter!'

Yana sneaked into the hall, stood in her usual spot, where she was hidden but could still make out the movement in the kitchen. Mom was attacking him back now, and she stood there listening as their relationship fell apart, because Yana knew they were hurting each other so deeply now that it would be irreparable. Yana heard things she'd never heard before, new accusations. Mom shouted that Dad had moved in with her against her will. She said he had forced himself on her that day. She never wanted this, she cried. One day he was just standing there with his fucking suitcases, she said, and they hadn't even discussed it.

'What the hell are you talking about?' Dad said.

'I never asked to share my life with you,' she replied.

Yana watched as Dad took a quick step towards Mom and shoved her so hard she fell to the floor, and there was a sudden silence, and now Yana realised he was going to kill Mom, and after that he would kill Yana. She turned around and dashed for the front door, sailed down the stairs and out to the street, ran for her life across the square in its Sunday torpor, onto the escalators to the subway, and just as she was about to hop the turnstiles she felt a hand on her back and there stood Dad, out of breath.

'Let's go back home and talk about this,' he said. And in silence they walked back the same way she'd run. He kept a hand on her shoulder all the while, and as they walked up the stairs she knew with certainty that she would enter the apartment and see her mother lying dead in the kitchen. She was so sure this was what must have happened, that he had killed Mom and then took off after her. But when they got home, Mom was just sitting at the kitchen table. And they didn't talk about it, Yana had to go to her room and Dad closed the door behind her so she wouldn't hear, and after a while he came in again and told her that he and Mom were going to take a walk, and behind him, in the hall, she saw Mom putting on a coat and placing a foot up on the chair to tie her shoes, and not once did she look Yana's way. Not even a glance. They went out, leaving her in the apartment. And Sunday crept along; she sat with Loser in her lap in the window seat, where she could keep an eye on the square, and at last she spotted Mom and Dad, they were walking slowly

155

back to the apartment, and when they came up they stood in her doorway. Mom took out three red slips, tickets, and said they were going to the circus that night.

The train slows down, and the meadows outside the window are covered in mist. It's still light out, but the sun will set any moment now. A gentle rain of yellow leaves on paved streets. She has arrived. The doors open and she disembarks onto the platform. She's the only one who gets off, and no one gets on. She walks across the narrow platform, stops by the sign. Malma Station. In front of it is the bench. It's been decades, but it's still there, it's the same bench. She opens the photo album to the photograph of her mother sitting on that bench with her face in her hands. She holds the picture up before her, trying to locate the spot where it was taken, and at last she finds it. The shiny rectangle is a magnifying glass into the past: she travels through a wormhole to 1976, and for a few seconds she experiences the whole thing in moving images, she doesn't take her eyes off the girl and her father. Yana watches as the girl stands up and walks right behind her father along the platform, away from the station. Where are you going? Yana follows them closely, hears the child breathing and anxiously clearing her throat, has to slow down so she won't step on the little girl's heels.

Chapter 13

Oskar

He feels the braking in his gut. So far there's nothing but open landscape on either side of the train; they're passing a pasture with an electric fence where three black horses gleam in the sunlight. Dust rises over a tractor driving on a gravel road between the crop fields. Red barns here and there, with half-hearted signs about farm sales or flea markets. He observes Harriet, who is leaning against the window, her forehead pressed to the glass.

'This is as far as we can go.'

That was how she put it yesterday, when she made it clear she didn't want to be with him any more. To him, this kind of suggestion is like an atomic bomb, it's not the kind of thing you can just say. He's never brought it up, not ever. But she does it all the time, every bad argument they have ends with her saying she's had enough, that she can't live like this. But yesterday was somewhat different, because she wasn't agitated. Calmly, collectedly, her eyes fixed on his, she informed him that it would be best for them to break up, and then she said, 'This is as far as we can go.' As though they had been on a journey, in constant motion, but facing ever greater resistance until they finally found themselves at a standstill. Time to get off the train.

He doesn't even know how it would work, to break up. He's never left anyone; in the few relationships he had in his youth he was always the one who got dumped. Not even when there were good reasons to break up has he been able to consider actually doing it. Near the start of his relationship with Harriet, he happened to see a text he wasn't supposed to. They were at the door and he was fumbling with his keys and her phone chirped. He noticed how quickly she put it away.

'Who was that?' he asked.

'Just a work thing,' she replied.

But he had seen it – it said 'Bornholm' on the screen. At first there was confusion that felt like a bad omen, and then he understood everything. That night he could think of nothing else and didn't get any sleep. The next day, he decided to forget about it, he shoved it aside and it lingered only as a vague sense of unease. That weekend he turned thirty-five, and when he came home at night Harriet had arranged a surprise party. Some friends were hiding in the apartment and jumped out once he'd taken a few steps into the hall. Bornholm was there, of course. The text he'd sent Harriet was to plan the surprise party. And that evening, when everyone had gone home, they lay in bed and she got to recount triumphantly how she had done it, how meticulously she had organised the whole thing, the web of secrecy! And Oskar told her he had actually seen a text from Bornholm and had gotten it into his head that she was having an affair. And they both giggled at that, and then they fell silent.

'But if you thought I was cheating,' she said, 'why didn't you confront me?'

He had no good answer. But the truth was, of course, that he would never leave her, no matter what she did.

'This is as far as we can go,' she'd said yesterday. Where she stands on that today, he doesn't know. She's hardly spoken at all on this trip, and even though she's the one who's cheating, he's the one who's sitting there fearing the consequences. And he's the one who has to come up with a plan, has to figure out what they must do to continue their life together. First and foremost, he must make sure Harriet feels better. She needs help, because there are stretches of time in which she simply doesn't function. One morning, *bam*, she won't get up and spends days in bed. He comes in to check on her sometimes, to ask if there's anything he can do; he calls the library and says she's sick, lies for her so she won't lose her job. And he hears her there in the bedroom, mumbling to herself: 'You are not alone, you are not alone.' Always that same incomprehensible mantra when she's underwater.

But it's not just about the two of them: he also has to find a way to get Yana back in the family. Harriet's love for Yana is insanely strong, almost like she wants to lay claim to her and shut Oskar out of it entirely. Those two have their own special relationship, but it's an unhealthy one and he has to keep tabs on it. So much of it is based on food and eating. Harriet is constantly obsessed with the idea of shoving junk food into Yana, and each time he protests, it only seems to spur her on: she wants to feed her more things, worse things. She uses food as a way to buy quick, cheap love from her daughter. Eating and drinking become a form of mischief the two of them have in common. Harriet will stand at the open fridge and whisper for Yana to come over, and, snickering, she'll pour her a glass of Coke for breakfast, but she has to drink it right there so he doesn't see. The sugar addiction she's spurred in Yana has taken on a life of its own, and he has to stop it. He sets rules about what Yana can eat, and Harriet sabotages them. It's creating a rift in the family. It takes Yana further and further from Oskar. He hates Harriet for it.

Oskar prepares to get off the train, throws the used cups of tea in the trash bag. Harriet is still doing nothing, just gazing out of the window. One time, after some make-up sex, she said they had to try to find their way back to what they once were. He wants to move on, move forward. What did she mean? Is it those first days of infatuation she wants to return to? He remembers that time as being full of uncertainty, never quite sure of where he had her. At some point, early on, he rented a car and picked her up in the late afternoon, honked when he saw her loitering outside her front door, dreaming, and she shoved her bag in the back, slamming doors and throwing herself into the seat beside him. It was still summer out, muggy August. They headed for the islands. The air conditioning bellowed, a few bottles of wine clinked against each other in a bag in the back. She put in a cassette tape and sang along, drumming the rhythm on her knees. That day was full of promise.

They got out of the car on the ferry and stood in the buffeting winds of the bow, their hair every which way, and they looked out at the water and she kissed him and he felt, as he so often did during those first days, that there must be some mistake. Why does she want to be with me? He remembers that the pilot up on the deck blew the horn and he looked up at the tinted glass and gazed out across the rows of cars gleaming in the sun, and the horn sounded again and Oskar knew he was honking at some other boat, but it felt like the pilot was saluting them, a greeting to the lovers there at the front. Then they drove on, the paved roads narrowing. These were his islands, he knew every single one of them, knew each curve before it appeared, and the small communities that were hardly even communities, just minor accumulations of houses. He could tell her stories about each of them. The trees thinned out, and they drove far out in the archipelago.

'Where are we going?' she asked.

'You'll see,' he replied.

The asphalt gave way to gravel, they passed nonchalant signs informing them that this land was 'PRIVATE', and suddenly the sea appeared, its enormity spread before them, and there, on a ledge down by the water, was a house with yellow wooden siding, two centuries old.

'Oh my God,' she said when he stopped the car outside.

'This is the most beautiful house I've ever seen. Who lives here?'

He fished a set of keys from his coat pocket. 'Tonight, that's us.'

She dashed into the yard, sending gravel sailing and flying about her feet, she laughed and screeched, and he stepped out of the car and looked up at the small estate, and right past it was nothing but deep blue, and he watched as she danced onto the stone steps, stood in the centre, equal numbers of windows on either side of her: it was symmetrical, it was balanced.

He had already shown this house to prospective buyers a number of times and knew it inside out, and now he wanted to guide her through the rooms, but she just hightailed her way through it and came out on the other side, down the slope where the rocks plunged straight to the sea. He grabbed a bottle of white and they settled down by the water. The wine glasses were unsteady on the rock. And the sun set over the islands. There was so little breeze that the whole bay was smooth, the cigarette smoke lingered above their heads. And they used their sweaters as pillows, gazed out at the islands and the small boats passing by, and there they lay in the twilight, making plans for their life together. If their first baby was a boy he would be called Benjamin, he said. But she knew it would be a girl, and she knew her name would be Yana, and he said, 'Yana? That's not a name.' And she replied, 'It is too a name. It's important to me for that to be her name.' And they lay there on the rock, tasting their daughter's name; she got up and shouted it across the water.

Then the August night came fast, all the lights went out in the depopulated archipelago, so they had no glow to bother them. It was an incredibly starry sky, the kind you only see a few times in your life. The house up above shone through the tall trees. A quick change. The Milky Way retreated; the night grew dark. They heard the sea gently begin to lap at a dock. A wind took tentative hold of the pines and a window up at the house banged shut. Shifting weather.

Giggling, they pulled each other up the steep slope, and they went to the bedroom and it was still so warm that they threw the windows open wide and the sky opened up, and they made love all night, again and again until the first birds shyly began to chirp at dawn. And they slept until late in the day, and as they headed back to the city he remembers thinking that this couldn't be real, *how did it happen?*, this shouldn't be possible, for her to be mine. They hadn't eaten breakfast, so they stopped at a fast-food joint. It was full of people, they ended up sitting right next to two teen boys, so close that it would have been strange if they didn't exchange a few words. She offered them a few of her salt packets when she noticed they'd forgotten to take any. Then one of the boys got out a plastic pack of sauce, tore the white lid off, and dipped his French fries in it. Harriet pointed at the sauce and told the boys it was the same colour as her labia. She mentioned it as if in passing, an amusing fact that had randomly crossed her mind. He could sense at once: that wasn't good. But she kept eating, all nonchalant, and the boys disappeared and after a while a security guard came up to ask what she had said to the children. She said she'd just been joking around a little. The guard asked her to exit the restaurant with him; he'd summoned the police and when Oskar saw a patrol car, lights on, turn into the parking lot he wasn't angry in the least, only bewildered. The police informed her that what she'd done was a sexual offence, but she couldn't take this seriously, she just laughed and shook her head as they questioned her. They let her go, and that same smile stayed on her face in the silence of the car and he couldn't look at her.

Those first days, first years – all the while he carried around that uncertainty about her. It was a relationship that took place entirely on her terms. When she got pregnant, a lot of things changed. All the conversations they'd had about children early on, the romantic and the real ones, as they dreamed about how it would all turn out as their duo became a trio. When she got pregnant, a forbidden thought came to him: now it would be harder for her to leave him. And it was true. She was the woman who always had her eye on the next thing, was always preparing to take off. Now she was stuck. One night, very early on in her pregnancy, she came home and confessed, sobbing, that she'd climbed onto a stone wall down by the shipyards and jumped off. Again and again she jumped, because she thought the baby would die, that it would all go away. But that panicked reluctance to be a mother vanished once Yana was born. Harriet just lay in bed being enamoured with her daughter. She loved Yana, she always had. They became homebodies, renting stacks of movies that stood on top of the TV. Harriet, standing in the kitchen and carefully chopping carrots and cucumbers into sticks, mixing her boring dip. And when they did go out, they no longer knew what to do. When they'd first met, she would always get so hammered. They did shots between courses, and he had to lead her home afterwards, calling out apologies to people she bumped into or insulted, or holding her hair back when she threw up on a lamppost. Now they sat silently in those same restaurants. They went home, the sound of her heels on the cobblestones. He had no issue with this – maybe the opposite, in fact. Their relationship had changed character, matured. This was the sort of quiet life that suited him. When Harriet says she wants to go back to what they once were, he nearly panics. He refuses to return to that time of no boundaries.

The train pulls into the station and Harriet stays put, looking out of the window. She's taken off her beaded bracelet and is fingering it, her thumb pressing bead after bead into her clenched fist, one pink, one blue, one pink, one blue, as though she wants to count them. When the train comes to a complete stop, she finally stands up. She smiles at Oskar as she passes him, and he follows her onto the platform. 'Harriet,' he says. He stops her and turns her to face him. He brushes away the hair that's fallen in front of her face and tucks it behind her ear. When they look at each other he feels a shiver from the past, from back in the beginning, when he couldn't meet her gaze, when he didn't know what to do with his own eyes. 'I'll do anything for you,' he says. 'I'm prepared to give you everything.'

She takes his hand, drops it after a moment. She walks towards the well-worn bench in the centre of the platform, right in front of the station building. She stands next to it, places a hand on the armrest, and lets her fingers run over the metal. She sits down in the centre of the bench, leans back. Their train slowly begins to move, and the bench is bathed in sunlight. She closes her eyes and just sits there, the wind in her hair and the oaks behind her fluttering and rustling in the breeze.

'Harriet,' he says.

She doesn't respond, because she's no longer there. She's travelled somewhere else, to a place he can't reach. He watches her as she sits there with her eyes closed, and he remembers something she told him once, a long time ago, the night he moved in with her, on her cramped balcony where you could see a sliver of the sea. The future has already been determined, it's impossible to influence, but what has already happened is changeable, always in motion. Maybe that's why she's clamped both hands on the bench as she sits, because the memories are in motion and she needs to hold on.

'I sat right here,' she says.

And then she says nothing more.

Chapter 14

Harriet

The train slows down and a voice on the loudspeaker says they're approaching Malma Station. 'Oh my God,' Dad says softly, and he closes his eyes, leans back in his seat. 'Finally.' Harriet has noticed that he's been disturbed by this trip, that he's grown more and more agitated. She has watched how he looks up at the loudspeaker in amazement each time the voice says that the next station isn't the one he was hoping for. Now she can relax, they've arrived. Dad would have much rather taken the car, but he can't. She doesn't really know what happened, but she does know it's her fault, that time last winter. Where were they going? She doesn't even remember, it was dark and cold out and the road was white and the snow was still falling as they drove and when the headlights shone into the dark the snowflakes reminded her of stars and it looked like the car was flying through the universe. And Dad drove with great focus on a road with lots of lanes then suddenly the whole inside of their car turned blue, lit up from behind by a flashing glow. A police car was right behind them, and the siren started to wail, it sounded plaintive in the wind. Harriet looked at the police car through the rear window and saw it flashing and ploughing through the whirling snow right behind them. 'Shit,' Dad whispered.

The patrol car pulled up beside them and now she would see them clearly, the blue lights on the roof, burning her eyes, and two police officers in front, a man and a woman. It was like a fairytale as they floated by, carried onward in their blue glow, hovering above the snow. The car swerved in front of them and they gestured at Dad to pull over and stop the car, and then they sat there on the hard shoulder, the police car way ahead of them, and Dad said 'shit' again, gripping the steering wheel in both hands until his knuckles went white. And the two officers got out and stayed at a distance for a moment, one of them made a note and disappeared into the patrol car again, but the other one, the man, approached their car slowly, and when he leaned in through Dad's lowered window everything in the car grew dark.

'You can turn off the engine,' said the officer.

'Why?' Dad asked. 'It'll get cold in the car.'

The policeman looked at Dad and leaned in a little more, wearing what might have been a smile. 'Could you please turn off the engine?'

Dad didn't move, he stared straight ahead into the darkness.

A few seconds passed, and then he turned off the car and everything went black, leaving only the blue lights of the car way up ahead.

'May I see your licence, please?'

Dad dug through his pockets and Harriet looked at the officer as he waited, and she saw the many pockets with different tools that hung around his waist, different buttons and taut leather over black metal, a row of dangerous things, strapped and secured and only the policeman himself knew how to handle all the risks he carried. The officer took out his flashlight so he could see the licence, and then he aimed the beam into the car and Harriet was blinded as it landed on her and she covered her eyes.

'Hi there,' the officer said to her.

'Hi,' she replied.

'Why are you doing that?' Dad asked. 'Why do you have to shine that on her?'

The policeman turned off the flashlight and tucked it away, then turned his eyes on Dad again. The same strange look, which she couldn't quite make sense of. A peculiar smile that maybe wasn't even a smile. 'I want to see who's in the car.'

The roar of traffic outside, and a cold wind from the open window, and the chafing silence from the policeman, as though he hadn't quite decided what to do with them. He handed the licence back to Dad. 'Do you know why we pulled you over?' he asked.

'Was I going too fast?'

'Indeed you were,' said the officer. 'Driving at such a

speed with a small child in the car, that's more than a little irresponsible.'

'Well, but . . .'

'And in these conditions to boot,' the officer said. 'On these icy roads.'

Dad didn't respond. The officer's tone made her nervous: you didn't talk to Dad like that. 'We followed you for a few kilometres. You didn't use your indicator a single time you changed lanes.'

'The road was empty, so I didn't think I needed to.'

'Was the road empty?' the officer asked. 'We were there, weren't we?'

The female officer came walking through the snow from the police car. She was in no rush, neither of the officers were, everything was happening so languidly, as though someone had slowed time. She approached the car and propped a hand on the roof and leaned in. 'This car is not road legal,' she said.

'Yes it is,' said Dad.

'No, you haven't had it inspected. Its indicators don't work and the brakes need attention.'

'The indicators work,' said Dad. 'A fuse went out, but they work.'

He started the car again and turned on the indicators, and the policewoman suddenly looked stern. 'Turn off the engine.'

'See?' Dad said. 'Do you see that they work?'

'Turn off the engine.'

The furious indicator light bled out over the drifts of snow to the right of the car. Dad turned it off.

'Where are you going, alone in the middle of the night?' the policewoman asked.

'I'm not alone. I've got my daughter with me.'

The policewoman quickly took out her flashlight and shone it into the car. Harriet was blinded by the beam again, held a hand in front of her face.

'Turn that off!' Dad shouted.

The woman aimed the flashlight at Dad, and his whole face turned white.

'Turn it off! For Christ's sake, turn it off!' Dad shouted.

'Get out of the car,' she said.

'What the hell?' Dad muttered. He slowly bent forwards, propping his forehead on the wheel. 'Can't you just leave us alone, just give me my goddamn ticket so we can get out of here someday?'

'Get out of the car,' the woman said again, and Dad shrank in his seat, holding tight to the wheel, staying put. Why didn't he do as she said? The policewoman simply opened the car door to haul him out, and everything became real, and it happened so fast. Now the officers' eyes were clear, their bodies tense, Dad didn't want to get out, and when the woman grabbed his arm he flailed to get free and his fist hit the policewoman's shoulder. Dad, who always knew before anyone else what would happen, who had always calculated everything beforehand. Now he knew nothing, couldn't control a thing as he was yanked out of the car and shoved to the ground. The policeman kneeled on Dad's shoulder, pressing him to the ground, and they started asking questions. These people who had been so laid-back at first, now they were in a hurry: quick movements and rapid-fire questions, without waiting for a response. 'Have you been drinking, have you taken any medication, do you have anything sharp on you?' Harriet leaned forwards, rubbed the fog from the window to see him. There was Dad, on the ground, still moving his legs a little but otherwise very calm now, he had given up. His cheek was pressed into the snow and he looked frightened, or maybe frightened was the wrong word. Harriet thought of a time she'd gone fishing with Dad and they pulled up a net and found perch and pike and she noticed that the fish dealt with their captivity in very different ways. The perch were grim, angry, ready to escape the second they got the chance, but she could hardly bear to look at the pike as they came up, with their open mouths and wide, sad eyes. They had given up. As Dad was about to kill the fish by severing their spines with a knife, he assured her that they felt nothing, understood nothing. And the perch went to their death grimly, faced it with wrath, a snap and they jerked and then it was over. But the pike. She saw the terror in their eyes, the fear of something that seemed worse than death. That's what Dad looked like as he lay there with his mouth open, his glasses askew, chewing the air like the pike. He was forever changed now.

It happened so fast, and she didn't have time to react before Dad was dragged off, over to the police car, and when she couldn't see him any more the car door on her side opened. There stood the female officer, who crouched in front of Harriet, smiled at her, and said, 'Come with me.'

A new direction.

Dad was driven off in one police car, and she in another. She doesn't know what happened to their car, did it stay there on the hard shoulder? They haven't ridden in the car since, but she thinks about it sometimes; she liked to sit in it because it reminded her of the time before the divorce, the times the whole family was gathered in it. The smell of Mom's cigarettes was still there. A piece of gum was stuck on the back seat, and when she scraped it with her nail and brought it to her nose she could still smell the mint, the scent of Amelia's breath. For her, the car was important, but even more so for Dad. She had seen how much he loved it, and he knew it so well, changed gears so smoothly and kindly, its rumbly engine that always started on the first try, even in the wintertime.

Dad hates trains, and that's why she's so relieved now: the journey is finally over for him. He gets up, checks under the seats for forgotten items. She gathers her markers, sorting them in order of colour in her case and putting it in her backpack. Outside the train window she can see that they're approaching a town, because the houses are closer together and the lawns are mowed here. He's in no rush, but Dad has begun to put on his boots; she sees the dried mud on their soles from all the birding expeditions she's never allowed to come on. He ties them meticulously and it takes a long time, and she can't explain it, it's almost like magic; he ties the last knot and is ready to go in the same instant the train stops at the station with a little jolt. He gets up and heads for the exit and Harriet follows, carrying the urn in the backpack and Dad's camera bag over her shoulder. They emerge onto a platform where the heat comes at them from the side, the sun right above the tall oaks. The platform is long and looks like a street; she follows Dad. A lone telephone booth on the platform. When the train leaves the station again, they're alone. Dad stops at a bench in the centre of the platform. 'Sit down here for a moment,' he says.

Harriet puts down the heavy camera bag and the backpack and sits on the bench, perched on the edge so her toes just reach the ground. He crouches in front of her. 'Before we go any further, I want to tell you what we're here to do.'

'Aren't we burying Bitty?'

'Yes, we're going to bury Bitty,' he says. 'But we didn't spend five hours on a train just for that.'

Dad takes off his glasses. When he squints in the sunlight, it sometimes looks like he's smiling. Harriet doesn't like this moment, she wants to know about things ahead of time, her stomach bothers her when she doesn't get the chance to prepare for what is about to happen.

'You've been here before,' Dad says. 'Do you remember?'

'No,' Harriet replies. She looks around, trying to spot a familiar building or a street that reminds her of something she's seen before.

'We came in a car that time, and it was dark.'

Harriet sees the old-fashioned lanterns that line the little street, and a memory turns up: what they looked like in the night, like moons hanging in a row, set out at intervals to lead

174

them the right way. A rain shower had just passed, wet asphalt gleaming in the car's headlights, and the smell of summer and soil coming through the open car window.

'Amelia,' Harriet said.

'Yes. She lives just over that hill,' Dad said, pointing up at the forest that rose over the station building. 'You're going to see her now.'

Chapter 15

Yana

Yana walks slowly along the platform, paging through the photo album, places it in her lap, the thin cellophane crinkling in the wind. She has followed Mom's train trip with her father. She sat on this bench, and then they moved on. Where did they go?

The next photo is a close-up of a bird sitting on a fence. It's hard to look at the picture. She found the photo album two days ago and has been wandering non-stop from page to page since, on the hunt for clues, but when the bird turns up she quickly flips the pages. She strongly dislikes birds, can't look into their eyes because there is only emptiness in there, nothing on the other side. Ever since she began working in the subway booth she's tried to avoid the night shift, because it means closing up the station and locking the doors – and one last task is to make sure to shoo out the birds that have come in from the square during the day. The pigeons hide in corners, you can only see them once you get up close, their black, shiny eyes gazing into eternity. Sometimes there are a lot of them, twenty-five or thirty, and she has to chase them with a broom, feathers in the air as she tries to herd them towards the exit. And they don't make a peep as they are herded out, silent as rats, just the sound of wing-beats in the night air. There is always one that has died and is still lying there. Yana can't touch a dead bird, so she uses newspaper to lift the dead bodies, and as she tosses them in the flower-beds she lets out a screech. Mom always made chicken on Saturdays, and the bird would spend the afternoon sitting on the counter like a white plastic soccer ball until she opened it up and began to prepare it in the evening. The naked legs and wings were slicked along the body, as though the creature had tried to shield itself or make itself small as it faced death. Mom stuffed things inside the bird, apples and carrots and spices, shoving vegetable after vegetable down its throat. One time Yana got up close and inspected the chicken, goosebumpy and full of flavour, ready for the oven, and she spotted bits of feather still on its breast: it had been sloppily plucked. She ran her fingertips over the sharp stubble, and after that discovery she could never go back, she never ate chicken again. And time after time she thought about quitting her job because she hated closing up when the birds had to go out, but she had no idea what other job she would do. And inside the glass booth, it was peaceful. She could read books there, and listen to the radio. She took shift after shift, the rumble as the trains passed beneath her lingered in her heels even after she got home. In the rush hour the passengers passed her in streams, time went quickly, but during the night shift it was a very different job, the sound of each new late-night traveller echoing down the hall. Drunken fights out on the square and loiterers detaching from the tile wall and approaching.

The day shift was always best. Most people simply walked by her, but on occasion someone wanted to ask a question and she would open the little window and the icy air outside would find its way in. These were conversations she could typically handle. Sometimes a commuter had forgotten their monthly pass or a teenager didn't have enough money to get downtown. She was typically generous, would close her eyes and quirk her head, in with you. But sometimes she could be brutal: for no reason at all, she might suddenly dress down someone who wanted to travel for free with a cruel comment.

One morning, a young man knocked discreetly on the glass; he was wearing a suit and a light coat. She opened her window and he seemed a little embarrassed, couldn't quite get the words out, and the morning rush was banging and rumbling behind him and someone was drilling through the cobblestones on the square and he had to raise his voice, saying he walked by each morning on his way to work. And he'd noticed her, he'd seen her sitting there every day gazing out at the subway entrance, and he said, 'You're so pretty when you're dreaming.' He said it so bashfully, although he had no reason to be bashful with that face! The man explained that he'd never done anything like this before – but would she be interested in getting a cup of coffee with him sometime? Or a glass of wine?

Yana had been floored by the question. She wasn't used to being asked out.

'Don't say no,' he cried when he realised she was hesitant. 'Say yes! Couldn't you just have a drink with me?'

With that, she had laughed and accepted, and when they planned a time to meet it turned out neither of them had any special plans that evening. He picked her up when she was done with her shift and they went to a Japanese restaurant on the square outside the subway station. He was a regular there, and he ordered for her. The dishes arrived plate by plate, soon every available spot on the table was full, and it felt generous, the way they ate on the continent, and they drank sake out of small ceramic cups, and it tasted like gasoline diluted with water. The drink was deceptive, transparent, and it felt like it evaporated before it hit your system, and both of them got drunk and giggly, and when the restaurant closed they were allowed to stay because he knew the owner, and as the staff cleaned up they sat side by side, looking out at the square. The 'T' sign for the subway lit up his face so that he looked pale.

'Why did you really ask me out?' she asked.

'I like girls like you,' he said.

'What kind of girl am I?' she asked with a laugh.

'A girl with something to grab onto.'

After that, they went to his place. He only lived a few blocks away. He poured red wine into tumblers and then disappeared into the bathroom and came out naked and asked if she wanted to shower together. She has a double memory of it: she felt both perfectly sober and drunk at the same time, the mood both serious and giggly. It was cramped, and they ran into things, hair-care products fell to the floor, and after a while he slipped and as he fell he grabbed the handle of the glass door, which hit the wall and shattered into a thousand pieces, the glass rained down on him and at first he laughed hysterically, but then he saw the blood flowing into the floor drain and he inspected himself and found a cut on his arm, the blood pulsing from the wound. 'Oh my God,' he said, and dashed for the medicine cabinet, trying to find something to stanch the blood; as he vanished from the bathroom, she heard cabinets opening and closing. He came back, now in jeans and a t-shirt.

'Don't move a muscle!' he cried. 'I'll be right back!'

'Where are you going?' she asked.

'I have to do something about this,' he cried shrilly, and he waved his injured arm at her. By now he was holding a hand towel over the cut, and it was red with blood. He flashed her a big smile, as though all of this had made him happy and exhilarated. 'Stay right where you are,' he cried. 'Don't go anywhere! I'll be right back!'

He disappeared and she started to laugh because it was all so surreal, and there was in fact something romantic about his words – all the blood notwithstanding, he didn't want to waste this moment. The door slammed and the apartment was quiet and she did as she'd been told. She wrapped herself in a towel and sat on the edge of the tub and waited for him.

181

After a while she got cold and emerged from the bathroom, gazed around at the apartment, small signs everywhere of a high standard of living. Electronics in the corners with little diodes blinking gently, welcomingly, a paper-thin computer monitor standing on nearly invisible feet on the desk. It looked like a suite in a luxury hotel; only the walls gave any indication that someone with a soul lived here: a framed and signed LP by an artiste she didn't recognise; photographs of a group of guys in various foreign locales tucked into the frame of a mirror. She followed the trail of blood he'd left on the floor: this is where he'd gone on the hunt for a bandage, red stains on the rug in the living room; here's where he ran to the kitchen, which was large and looked almost industrial with its small kitchen island and barstools, and she could picture herself there. She could imagine what it would be like to live with him in this apartment, sleep in that bed, eat breakfast in that kitchen. With him. Everything felt familiar and safe and obvious, and she found herself thinking of the time her mother had sat on the edge of her bed to have a talk about boys with her, had said that true love always comes out of nowhere, when you're least expecting it, and when it happens you won't hesitate, you'll just know: this is it.

After waiting for another hour or so, she got dressed again, sat down on the edge of his bed, and waited some more, and outside the light grew milky as it does when dawn is coming, and when she saw the first rays of sun come over the rooftops across the street she got up and went home. She doesn't know what happened, where he went, but the most likely explanation is: he went to the emergency room at Söder Hospital and had to wait for hours before they stitched him up. Before she left, she memorised his last name from the letter-box and later found his mobile number, and that same night she texted him: 'Sorry, I know I promised to wait in the bathroom, but I couldn't wait FOR EVER ...' and then, immediately, another text: 'But please do try again sometime.'

After that, she carried her phone close but never got a response, and there was something about that whole night, how he had simply disappeared, the growing mystery, and how he never answered, that did something to her. She couldn't stop thinking about him. The next day she called the number but got his voicemail, and she heard his voice, that confident cheerfulness, that bubbliness, when you can hear in one word the next word forming, and she saw his smile before her as she heard it, and she was right back there with him at the Japanese restaurant, his big laugh, so silly and confident as he tucked a napkin into his collar before he ate.

This is it.

She called and called, and after a week she stopped calling. But she was still helplessly caught up in thoughts of him. That was a long spring.

Nowadays, when she went to work, she got off at the station before the one she worked at and walked the last little bit, because that way she could go by the apartment building where he lived. She thought that she would eventually run into him there, as he was on his way in or out. She slowed down as she approached the building, glancing up at his apartment on the second floor for signs of life. She walked by twice a day all through that cold spring, but she never saw him, and in the evenings she mostly stayed at home, stuck in a frustration she'd never experienced before, a feeling that bordered on despair or even some sort of fury. She sometimes had outbursts. She destroyed things in her apartment, throwing books at the wall or breaking teacups in the sink. Sometimes, in the midst of her tears when she sat at home despairing, she also felt something else, a bit of pride about having these feelings. It was a big deal to be capable of them, of having all of this inside you.

She daydreamed about him, and as she sat in her glass booth she gazed out at the streams of passengers each morning to see if he was somewhere in the crowd. After all, he'd told her he passed by here every day – but now she never saw him. A suspicion came to her, one she couldn't shake. Her subway station had two entrances, one on either end of the platform, and one morning she asked the woman who worked in the glass booth on the other side if she would consider switching with her, just for one day. And she sat down in her new glass booth and gazed out at the morning commuters beelining for their workdays, and after a while she saw him, there he was. His quick steps, his face always close to a smile, his hand inside his jacket as he looked for his subway card. Yana quickly opened her little window and called out to him, and her heart pounded through her snug jacket, and he turned to her with a smile as though he was immediately glad to see her. He waved at her in passing and vanished down the escalator.

And that was that.

She had found him out, but she was the one, not him, who was humiliated.

Yes, that was a long spring, but of course it passed. Eventually, she felt nothing. All things come to nothing, feelings included. Sometimes she happens to think of him and how important and crucial it all felt with him, and then it no longer meant anything.

That bracelet she made for Mom at the pool, it had once meant everything. A few weeks after Mom disappeared, Dad came into her room and handed it to her. 'Maybe you'd like to keep this,' he said.

Yana had put on the bracelet and decided it to wear it for the rest of her life. It was her most important possession, but after a few months it broke when they were playing inne-bandy at school, and she got down on all fours and cried and picked up the beads. She would find every last one, and fix the bracelet. She placed the beads in a bowl that she kept on her desk at home. But she never bought a new string to put the beads on, so they just sat there for a few years and then they were gone; she doesn't know where they went. Maybe Dad tossed them. They were so important to her, that bracelet had been everything, and then it was nothing.

And the same goes for this photo album; for the moment it's more important than anything else, following its trail, but she supposes there will come a time when it fades into oblivion as well, when this train trip will have lost its colour and the photo album will lie there on some shelf like an inexplicable nothing. She looks down at the photograph of the bird, and tastes blood in her mouth once again.

On the facing page is another picture, a photo that's darker than the others. It's underexposed, but all the details are plainly visible in deep hues. A clearing leading to a shady forest. The colours do odd things, hints of sunlight glittering over black trees, but at the same time it looks like harsh dusk above, the sky ice-cold, deep blue. On the right side of the picture is the man who must be Mom's father, Yana's grandfather. A dark figure at the edge of a dark forest. His expression is grim. It's as though he was moving towards the camera to keep the picture from being taken. Dark eyes, half-open mouth. She doesn't like the look of him.

Yana closes the album and gazes out at the little street that runs alongside the rail line. Past it is the forest, where she's going. She sees the tall pines rise like a wall along the road, and for the first time on this journey she wonders if it would be best to turn back, because it's not a good idea to look for something you're not sure you want to find. She can't shake the vision of her grandfather's expression. His worried eyes, his hounded appearance. He looks like a man who has just been through something harrowing out there in the forest.

Chapter 16

Oskar

Harriet is no longer reachable. She's in her childhood again; by now he's learned her ways and can see in her eyes that there's no point in even trying. It's like she fumbles ahead with her gaze turned inwards, tentatively feeling her way around before she decides which parts she can revisit and which she should let be.

'I sat right here,' she says, placing her hands on the black metal.

He sits down beside her on the bench. She takes a photograph from her purse and shows it to Oskar; it's Harriet as a girl. She's standing in front of this bench, at this train station, a long time ago. She's looking directly into the camera, smiling yet clearly seconds from tears.

'Is this from your trip here?'

'Yes. I found it in a photo album Dad and I put together after the trip.'

'Why are you so sad?'

'Dad took a picture of me even though I didn't want him to.'

Oskar looks at the picture, and it cuts right through him. He observes her eyes and her expression; it's the instant before a child breaks down. Harriet is standing there with her father, yet she is entirely alone at that station. Her father doesn't give her a hug when she's upset, he takes a picture of her instead. Oskar closes his eyes. Childhood is a mystifying installation, like a piece of modern art. Baffling and unnecessary. You just want to kick the whole shitty thing to pieces.

The breeze comes and goes, making awnings flap and slamming an open window closed against the deserted street. The platform is empty and the summer is oppressive.

'Do you know when I fell in love with you?' she asks.

'No.'

'Why haven't we ever talked about it? It was the day we went up to see my childhood home,' she says. 'Remember?'

He laughs. 'Yeah, you were sick with a fever. We sat on the balcony all night.'

'Ask me anything about that night on the balcony. I went to the bathroom, and when I came out you were waiting for me just outside, in the hall. I was taken aback, I had no idea what you were doing. You said it was such a waste of our time for me to walk all the way back to the balcony on my own. You wanted to make the most of our time.'

He shakes his head and smiles.

'What?' she asks.

'So corny.'

'It was the nicest thing anyone had ever said to me,' she says.

'Then we kissed,' says Oskar. 'And I asked you: is it you and me now?'

'And I answered: Now it's you and me.' She takes out her pack of cigarettes, bends forward, lighting it down low so it won't go out in the wind.

'Tell me what happened here,' he says.

'Can't we just sit here for a while?' is her response.

She holds the cigarette with the very tips of her fingers. Once she told him that she likes to smoke into the wind. He stored this in his memory for some reason, and now he happens to think of it, smoking into the wind, and he feels the urge to mention it to her but then the urge passes.

'That night on the balcony you told me something from your childhood,' she says. 'That you longed for your mother's touch.'

'Yes, she wasn't much of a hugger.'

'Tell me more about her.'

'I hardly remember her.'

'Of course you do,' she says.

'Eh,' he replies. 'I've told you about her. She was just nuts.'

'How so?'

'I can tell you one thing I do actually remember,' he says, feeling a little burst of energy as though he's just realised something important. 'I always used to get lost when we were shopping in a big grocery store. Suddenly Mom would be gone and I would walk around crying. But one of those times, when I was desperately looking for her, I caught sight of her. She was behind the vegetable counter – hiding.' He reaches for Harriet's cigarette and she hands it over. Her lipstick on the filter; he takes a drag, smokes into the wind. 'Do you get it?' he asks. 'She hid over and over again, on purpose, because she wanted to watch me walking around, crying and looking for her. She got a kick out of seeing me so upset, a kick out of being the one who eventually rescued me.'

'Jesus Christ,' she says.

'Yeah,' Oskar replies. He laughs, brings his hand to the top of his head to smooth his mop of hair. 'I'm telling you. Mom was a little nuts.'

'A little nuts,' Harriet says softly. 'That's more than a little nuts. That's the kind of thing that shapes a person.'

'Oh?' he says. 'I never thought that sort of thing would matter.'

'Once when I was little, I was lying in bed listening to my parents talking in the kitchen,' she says. 'They had decided to get a divorce and they were going to split us girls up. Both Mom and Dad wanted Amelia, but neither of them wanted me. I live with that conversation every day. I'm a reject. I always have been, always will be.'

He puts his arm around her and she rests her head against his chest, and then she's gone again, back through the decades. That's where Harriet thrives. The straight lines from her childhood until the present day; all the things you are now can and must be explained by something that happened in the past. Sometimes he's jealous of the security she finds in that banality, so sure of all these links. It must be so simple

190

to live that way, because there's an answer for everything, everything has an explanation! And you're never to blame for anything, you're merely a perpetual victim of other people's faults and shortcomings.

'Is that why you always want to know where I am?' Harriet suddenly asks.

'What?' Oskar says. He sits up and looks at her.

'All those times in the grocery store,' she says. 'Is that why you call me twenty times a day? Is that why you always want to know where I am?'

'What are you talking about?'

'You're afraid that I'm going to run off too?'

'Stop it,' he says. 'Let's go.'

He gets up and notices that she recoils from him, frightened by his sudden movement. And something flashes in her eyes and then disappears as she realises he's only standing up. What was that he saw? Fear? Did she think he was going to hurt her? She once told him she doesn't like it when his eyes go black; she doesn't want to be near him when that happens. In recent days he's noticed that he's increasingly ending up in that state where he's paralysed by rage. His vision narrows, he sees blood-red dots when he closes his eyes, sounds are distorted, laughter sounds like squealing pigs, loud noises are intolerable. It doesn't take much, just some small thing going awry: when he asks Yana to buy vacuum bags from the store and she comes back with the wrong kind. When they have a glass of wine at night and he takes out the wine glasses, he sometimes finds stains from Harriet's lipstick on the rims, still there even though the glass has been washed and is otherwise clean, and when he sees that fat red lip-print he is so inexplicably triggered.

Some afternoons he comes home for a nap. He might sleep for hours and wake to find it's evening and Harriet is returning home from work. Is he depressed? They went to France for New Year, against his wishes: why should they go there to freeze? The colossal hotel right on the boardwalk, glowing brilliantly from far off – they'd spotted it even from the air as they were coming in for landing, and they'd pointed and exclaimed. But as they entered the lobby, the heavy mood hit them, a doorman stood at the revolving door, looking dejected. Long days in the rain, playing cards in the lobby, the hotel owner sometimes appeared at the reception desk, sat there disdaining his guests for staying at his shabby hotel. On New Year's Eve there was a 'gala dinner', and they got dressed up so they could have a crappy time in the hotel ballroom alongside all the other guests. As it grew close to midnight, the staff ran around handing out glittery party streamers and hooters with which to announce oneself when the clock struck twelve. And Oskar blew on his and there was something deeply melancholy about the sound that came out. He honked and honked, and the sad sounds rang out from the other tables too, and he thought they sounded like desperate calls for help from other unhappy families, and he blew more and harder and the table next to theirs answered, a cacophony of *Weltschmerz*, and he couldn't stop laughing at how bizarre it was; he kept blowing and laughing as Harriet and Yana looked at him in amazement because eventually he couldn't breathe. He couldn't stop laughing, and afterwards when they went back to their room to go to bed and he pulled the curtains, which smelled of water damage, Harriet said to him, 'I can't even remember the last time I heard you laugh.'

Is Yana afraid of him? Is that why they're drifting ever further apart? One time he discovered her eating burnt matches in front of the TV. He told her to stop. She kept doing it in secret, clumsily hiding the evidence, leaving gnawed stumps of matches around the apartment. Oskar gathered a few of them, called her into the kitchen. He told her enough was enough. Don't eat matches. Period. She was so shaken that she started crying. 'Oh, sweetie,' he said, and hugged her. He felt her heart beating as he embraced her, felt her whole body shaking. Why? What does he do to make her so scared? He never even raises his voice. Except in extreme circumstances.

He went into her room the other day to collect the dishes there, and she had set a teacup on the bookcase, and there he also caught sight of a hundred-kronor bill. It was hidden behind some toys and folded a few times so it wouldn't be visible. It had never occurred to him that his daughter might steal money from him. He was known to brag about her to friends, saying that Yana had a strong moral compass, she always knew right from wrong. When Yana got home from school that afternoon, she went straight to her room and Oskar followed close on her heels. He pointed at the money on the bookcase. 'Where did this money come from?' he asked.

Yana looked at him quizzically.

He picked up the bill and held it up. 'Where did you get a hundred kronor from?'

'It's not my money.'

'Then whose is it?'

'I don't know.'

'You don't know?'

Yana sat down on the edge of the bed and looked at the floor. Oskar sharpened his tone, told her he wanted the truth: where did the money come from?

She said someone gave it to her.

'First you don't know where it came from,' said Oskar, 'and now you say someone gave it to you. Which one is it, Yana?'

'Someone gave it to me.'

'Who?'

Yana didn't respond, and Oskar struck a wooden box on the bookcase full-force, causing it to fly off the shelf and hit the wall behind her. '*Do not lie to me!*' he shouted.

Yana offered no further protest, just sat in silence on the edge of the bed, refusing to make eye contact.

'You stole money from me and that makes me fucking furious,' Oskar said. 'But what makes me even more furious is your lies.'

And it happened again: she burst into tears, she sat there shaking, and the beginnings of words came from her mouth, but he wasn't about to go easy on her just because she regretted her actions. He took away her phone and headed for the door, and before he closed it behind him he said, 'You may not leave this room until I say you can.'

Nothing but silence from her room all that afternoon, and in the evening Harriet returned home and Oskar told her what had happened and that Yana was banished to her room without her phone to think about what she'd done. Harriet thought this was a reasonable punishment, but Oskar was already having second thoughts, because what kind of consequence was this for someone who spends all her time in her room in the first place? When dinner was ready, Oskar summoned Yana and she ate in silence, not saying a word to either Oskar or Harriet, and when she was finished she curtly offered the customary 'thanks for dinner' and disappeared back into her room.

'Is *she* angry now?' a surprised Oskar said to Harriet.

It would take a few days for everything to be cleared up.

At the circus the day before, Harriet had gone to the bathroom while Oskar took Yana to buy some popcorn. When he opened his wallet, he paid with the hundred-kronor bill he'd found in her bookcase. He smoothed out the tightly folded bill and handed it to the popcorn seller and, as he fiddled with it, Yana stared at it.

'I didn't steal that from you,' she said.

'There's no need to discuss it any further,' Oskar said.

'I didn't steal it.'

'Then where did it come from?'

'I got it from that man at the pool when we were having a snack. He gave it to me to buy candy. But I was afraid to tell you so.'

She took her popcorn and they went into the big top to

find their seats. He placed a hand on her shoulder, and it felt awkward and unfamiliar, and she stiffened.

When do you lose your child?

Harriet takes one last drag from her cigarette and stubs it out on the bench, then tosses the butt onto the tracks. She stands up and walks along the platform; they pass a small kiosk, yellow and black news-sheets. 'USA AT WAR WITH TERROR.' She walks faster, as though she's suddenly in a hurry. He catches up with her.

'Where are we going?' Oskar asks. 'What are we doing?'

'We're going to dig up a grave,' she replies.

Chapter 17

Harriet

The bench is warm in the sunshine, almost burning her through her thin black dress. Dad crouches before her and places a hand on her knee. When he says she's going to see her sister, her only response is, 'Huh?' And she immediately regrets saying it, because what if she heard wrong and he's about to say something totally different?

'You're going to see your sister.'

For a moment she gazes at her father with suspicion, and she opens her mouth to say something but no words come out, and she feels sad. She's happy too, she must be, because today is the day she gets to see her sister, but more than anything else she feels sad, because it's as if all the days she hasn't seen Amelia are tumbling down on top of her. She knows how Dad feels about crying and she's determined not to let it happen, but each time she feels Dad's hand on her shoulder, the tears get a little closer. She covers her eyes, sits there looking into her palms. And in the red darkness she tries to concentrate, think about fun things, to keep herself from crying. Suddenly she hears the sound of Dad taking a photo and looks up. He's taken a few steps back; he lowers the camera and looks at her.

'May I take a picture of you?' Dad asks.

'Yes,' she says, clearing her throat. She stands up, looks at the camera, and hopes he'll snap a photo quickly, before she has time to start crying. He fiddles with his settings and she has to check herself, try to keep it all inside. He takes another picture.

'Sorry,' he says. 'But you're just so lovely.'

'It's OK.'

He puts the camera back in the bag. He looks up at her again, maybe with something else in his eyes, a guilty conscience? 'You can make a photo album of this trip when we get home,' he says. 'Won't that be fun?'

Dad walks along the platform and she follows on his heels; he's walking on the safety line, as though it's a game, balancing on the white stripe without touching the asphalt, and she likes that and follows him along the line, like a tightrope walker, but it turns out it was only a coincidence, he wasn't playing. Now he's walking alongside the line. She follows him. They cross the tracks and wander along the other side, on the small, paved street that's lined with shops on the ground level of the apartment buildings. Someone has graffitied the façade: 'USA OUT OF VIETNAM.' She knows Dad agreed with that. And then up the small road that vanishes into the forest.

'Dad,' she says. 'Does Amelia know we're coming?'

'No,' he replies, and his tone sounds surprised, as though this was a stupid question, as though it's obvious she doesn't know.

'What will Mom say?' Harriet asks.

Dad doesn't respond.

'Dad,' says Harriet. 'Mom doesn't want me to see Amelia.'

'No, she does,' says Dad. 'Of course she does, really.' He looks at his watch. 'Mom won't be home.' He stops, bends down towards her and places a hand on her shoulder. 'And if she is at home, I'll handle it.'

Harriet doesn't know what that means. She doesn't like the images that play in her mind: Mom upset and shouting and Dad handling it. She hadn't even thought about Mom during this whole walk from the train station, not until now, as she's walking through the woods and looking around for something that's familiar to her from that summer day. It's been a year since she was here. Mom who was no longer Mom in that kitchen, talking in a new way, wearing different clothes, saying strange things. That peculiar chill.

Up the hill, evergreen forest on either side of the road, and suddenly there's a glimpse of a memory she had stored somewhere: a tiled roof towering high. She rested her eyes on those tiles for hours during that long afternoon. Glitter between the tree trunks; there's the lake. And the brick house she saw for the first time in darkness, the yellow glow from its windows. There it is now, silent in the sun, white as a church. The dock is still down by the lake and there are signs of people there, bathing trunks draped over the timber posts to dry. They pass the fence where she sat to wait for her father, as the sun crossed from one side of the sky to the other that day. Dad stops: a bird is perched on the fence. He says it's a robin redbreast, and he asks Harriet if she remembers how the redbreast got its name. She says she does, and he's satisfied. He takes a picture of the bird and they walk on, through the gate; they pass a sundial, a circle of black wrought iron that's held up by a sculpture of a naked boy. Harriet feels a wave of uneasiness; if Mom had hired lawyers who said Amelia and Harriet weren't allowed to see each other, are they allowed to be here in their yard?

Dad walks up onto the wooden deck, past the oil-finished deck furniture, and rings the doorbell. He leans near the window and cups his hands to peer in. She doesn't understand how he can be so bold. He looks at his watch. 'Amelia should be home from school any minute,' he says. 'We can wait for her here.' He sits down on a lawn chair that's facing the lake. Beside it is a patio swing, which looks delightful. She sits on it and sinks deep into the soft, sun-warmed fabric. Her feet just barely reach the ground.

'Damn strange colour on that lake,' Dad says, gazing out.

'Green,' Harriet says.

'Silt,' Dad says. 'That's what happens when the water in a lake doesn't move. It's perfectly still.'

It's so hot, and the sun is low enough to shine in under the canopy of the swing. She hears some birds close by, and

200

Chapter 18

Yana

It wasn't very difficult. The photograph of the bird on the fence, the silhouette of a white house behind it. And then the picture of Harriet as a child, sitting next to a small tree, a lake behind her, and a dock. When you search 'Malma' on Google Maps, there's only one body of water nearby, a small lake. And around that lake is only one house, and that's where she's headed. She walks alongside the tracks, and it's late afternoon, getting dark. She walks under moon-shaped streetlights that make the asphalt shimmer, shiny maple leaves plastered to the pavement. She sees the small road that leads in among the trees, it's darker here. The forest is quiet, just something trickling, water under moss, between the rocks. Up on the hill, she gazes out across the forest in its different shades of blue, and there's a streak of mist on the lake. She sees a low-slung house, it crouches near the earth. No lights are on in the house, it doesn't look like anyone's home. The house is made of sand-lime bricks.

She remembers a subway trip one time, on her way to a Hallowe'en party at the home of a guy in her class, on the red line, further than she'd gone before. It was a costume party, and she had dressed up as a witch, a pointy hat on her head and a long black dress she'd found in Mom's wardrobe, among the clothes she'd left behind. She had to lift it as she walked to keep the hem from dragging on the ground. And she walked among the houses in the rain, rows of single-family homes made of sand-lime brick, houses that looked so inviting, with up-to-date lighting on their patios, lights sticking up from small holes in the wooden-slat floors, illuminating the moisture trembling in the air. She peered into those houses and saw no anguish anywhere: happy families spending time together, conversations around kitchen tables, preparing meals, TVs on, a father dashing around and playing with a young son. She was walking on happy streets. And then she rang the doorbell at her classmate's house, and as she waited she rested a hand on the white façade, she imagined that the brick would be warm. But of course it wasn't. An immediate wave of confusion as the door opened; it was her classmate's mother, who saw her drooping hat and called anxiously to her son, who soon turned up behind her. He wasn't wearing a costume. 'Didn't they let you know?' the mom said. 'Didn't you hear that the party was cancelled?'

No, she hadn't heard. Something had gone wrong, a telephone tree that didn't make it all the way, and she was the only one who hadn't been reached with the news that the party was cancelled because the rain would keep them from being outside. 'You can't just go home now that you've come all this way,' the mom said, and invited her in. They sat in the kitchen and the mom made a pitcher of fruit drink and looked in the freezer for some cinnamon buns, which were soon rotating in the microwave, and the guy from her class joined her at the table even though Yana suspected he thought it was annoying. And his dad came down, surprised, placed a hand on his son's shoulder as though this were a perfectly natural thing to do, and asked what was going on.

'Oh no!' he cried. He looked unhappy. 'How idiotic.'

Yana had taken off her hat but felt ridiculous in her over-long and clingy black dress, but the guy from her class, who she'd never been brave enough to talk to, he just sat there looking friendly and smiling at her.

'How will you get home?' the mom asked. 'Should I call your mother?'

'No, I'm OK,' Yana replied.

Then she took off again, the family said goodbye to her in the hall as food simmered on the stove, and she walked back to the subway, past the long row of sand-lime brick houses.

She's close now. Dusk is falling fast, but she can still see the dock down by the lake and right next to the shore is a gigantic tree, apples scattered on the ground around it. She takes a few steps down the grassy slope, but then she hears sounds from the deck of the house. There, in the dim glow, she sees something. Is that a person sitting there? She sees the shadow of something, a small movement.

'Hello,' Yana calls. There's no reaction from the house. She takes a few steps closer to the building. 'Hello,' she calls again.

'Yes, hello, hello,' comes a voice.

Yana takes a few more steps towards the house, and now she can see that an older woman is sitting there. She's sunken into a porch swing on the deck and is rocking it gently. Yana stops at a respectable distance, doesn't want the woman to feel threatened.

'I'm sorry,' Yana says. 'I didn't see you, I didn't think anyone was home.'

'Are you the one who graffitied the military barracks up in the forest?'

'Graffitied the military barracks? No, that wasn't me.'

'It was someone,' the woman says. She coughs and looks for the handkerchief that's in her lap, coughs into that. 'It's so warm inside,' she says. 'I told them to turn down the heat, but nothing happens.'

Yana looks at the house, notices that the woman has left the door wide open. A TV is on in the living room, and it lends a faint glow to the room, she sees a lone easy chair facing the screen.

'I'm sorry to just barge in like this. That dock down there, does it belong to you?'

'How should I know?' the older woman says. 'My daughter will be here soon. I'm sure she'll be able to answer.'

'Don't you live here?' Yana asks.

'Of course I live here,' the woman replies, staring at her in astonishment. 'Who did you think lived here?'

A low rumble from the train station reaches the house, a train that doesn't stop, just passes swiftly through the forest, and then all is quiet again. The woman listens carefully, gazing out at the universe, and then she loses interest. 'My daughter will be here soon,' she says. 'She's with the horses, I think. But she'll be in a car, she never takes the train.'

'I'm here on sort of a special errand,' Yana says. 'It's a long story, which won't interest you, but I'm wondering if it would be OK with you if I dug something up down by the lake, something I think my mom buried a long time ago.'

'So silly,' the woman says.

Yana tries to see her, but it's too dark, there's only her faint silhouette on the big swing. 'What's silly?' Yana asks.

'It's not good to carry on like that,' the woman says. 'It's not good to go digging in the past.'

Yana passes her on the deck.

'What's done is done,' she hears the woman say. Her voice is shrill and mewling. 'No use dwelling on it!' she cries.

'No, of course,' Yana says.

'I only look forward,' she says, gesturing at the lake with her whole hand. 'I work at a bank. But the banks just keep closing and they keep moving me around, now I have to go 120 kilometres every day to get to work. Do you know how many hours I spend in a car each year?' She starts laughing and then coughing, and in the middle of a cough she shrieks: 'I spend my entire life in a car!' She continues to cough but after a while she falls silent, wipes her mouth with her sleeve.

Yana can't make this add up. The woman is well past retirement age, she must be seventy-five, if not older. Could she still be working at a bank?

'I wouldn't ask if it weren't important,' Yana says. 'May I dig in your yard?'

'Go right ahead,' the woman replies.

'I promise to put everything back the way it was.'

'Sure, sure.'

'Do you have a shovel I could borrow?'

'No,' she replies. 'No shovels here.'

Yana looks around and immediately spots a shovel leaning against the garden shed. She walks over and holds it up for the old woman. 'Look,' Yana says.

'Yes, you can use that.'

Yana sets her sights on the lake, and as she walks by the woman she can't help but cast a quick glance at her.

'Do you know my daughter?' the woman asks as Yana walks by.

'No, I'm sorry.'

'She's a good girl. But she can't fix the heat. I don't understand why it would be so difficult.'

Yana heads down to the lake; it's steep and the grass is wet and slippery.

'What's her name?' calls the woman from up by the house.

Yana stops and turns around. She sees the older woman on the swing, now sitting perfectly still.

'Who?' Yana calls back.

'My daughter,' says the woman, and then there's a softer

mumble that Yana can hardly make out, as though she's mostly talking to herself. 'What is her name?'

The reflection of the heavens on the lake. There's the apple tree. In the photo the tree is very small, and now it's enormous. She places the shovel at the base of the trunk and pushes. The blade sinks smoothly into the soil. She digs in the dark.

Chapter 19

Oskar

As they walk by the Malma Station building, Oskar notices a sign on the wall that gives the distance in kilometres, down to the decimal point, to a number of nearby towns. That's right, the only interesting thing about this community is how far it is to somewhere else. They walk down a small shopping street that runs parallel to the train tracks; he's never been here before, yet he has been here a thousand times. He grew up in a town just like this one, and he knows everything about it. She stops outside a bakery.

'I need a bite to eat,' Harriet says, and walks in. They grab a tray and he slides it along past the empty steel counters. There's condensation on the glass, a few baked goods and a plate of plastic-wrapped roll sandwiches. She selects one with cheese, the tray slides silently on towards the cash register.

'I don't think that was made fresh today,' Oskar says softly, but Harriet isn't interested. She picks out a soda as well, and the short lady at the register places a hand on the bottle before she accepts payment, to check if it's cold. The lady is familiar with her useless cooler. They sit down at the small table by the window, facing the street. She fingers the plastic around her sandwich.

'It's so crazy that we're here,' she says, looking out at the street and the train station beyond. 'Dad wouldn't believe it if he knew.' She removes the slice of pepper from her sandwich and the impression of it remains, sudden evidence of the cheese's original colour beneath.

'Do you miss him?' Oskar asks.

'Eh,' she says. 'I think about him a lot. Sometimes I dream about him.'

'What kind of dreams?'

'You know, there's something I think about so often, but I haven't been able to bring myself to tell you. Dad was wearing a pulsometer at the hospital, remember that?'

'No,' Oskar says.

'Yeah, it beeped every time Dad's heart beat. And I remember that in the minutes before he died, his heart beat slower and slower until it stopped. For all my life I thought it would be the other way around. I always thought when a body was failing the heart would beat faster and faster until it collapsed somehow. That the heart would, like, beat itself to pieces.'

Oskar laughs. 'That's what you thought? I think you might be alone in that.'

'Anyway, I think that way would be nicer. One last

explosion, so you disappear at full speed. Instead of that slow, blurry sort of end.'

It's true that Bo's death didn't happen the way anyone would have imagined. At first there was urgency, urgency in the taxi, after the hospital called to say Bo had been in an accident. But when they arrived, time just passed more and more slowly. They learned that Bo had crashed on his bicycle. Harriet had had the feeling something would happen with that bike. One time, Oskar was walking downtown with her and Bo suddenly came over a rise at full speed, crouched over the handlebars, no helmet on his head. The old man who was determined not to be an old man. He was invincible, untouchable, nothing could ever happen to him. Harriet had called out to him on the street and he had stopped, their brief conversation amid the noise of traffic, both gazing at the pavement as they spoke. They hadn't seen each other in a few years. And after a while, she said, 'Please, Dad, can't you wear a helmet when you're cycling?'

'Yeah, yeah.'

'I worry about you,' she said. 'I don't want you to get hurt.' She placed her hand over his.

'Bitty,' he said.

'Bitty.'

When Harriet saw her father in the hospital bed she dashed over to him, but at first she was afraid to touch him because she didn't know where he was hurt. She just sat close to him. Bo looked at her with what appeared to be a smile, but when Harriet tried to talk to him there was no response.

A doctor came in and didn't say much, just a few words full of vast amounts of information. 'Your father has suffered a serious brain injury. The pressure inside his skull has increased very rapidly. There is no chance of saving his brain with an operation. We have moved to palliative care. That means we won't be pursuing any life-saving measures. He can see and hear you, but he can't speak.'

She sat on the edge of his bed and ran her hand over his hair, and she cried. Between her sobs, she kept repeating the same thing: 'My sweet little daddy.' This man, who was so enormous, whose colossal shadow had loomed over Harriet all her life — suddenly he was her sweet little daddy. She placed her hand on his cheek and Bo, unable to produce even a single word, looked at her with an expression that almost resembled curiosity. There were brief attacks of confused rage from Harriet, which she directed at nurses or doctors. 'How can you just give up? He's alive! You have to do something!' It probably had to do with the fact that he appeared intact, not to mention that he was sitting nearly upright and his gaze was clear. And yet: there was almost no activity here. A nurse stood in a corner, as though she didn't want to disturb them, sometimes approaching to check some value on a small screen.

Harriet leaned over to inspect the back of her father's head and let out a scream and looked away. 'What have you done,' she whispered. 'Sweet little Daddy, what have you done?'

And maybe it was when she'd seen what had happened to his head that she understood, because after that there were no more protests. Bo lay there in his own clothes. Someone had cut open his shirt, maybe to see if there were injuries elsewhere on his body. The nurse approached with a syringe and injected it into his arm. 'We're giving him morphine constantly,' the nurse whispered. 'So he doesn't feel any pain, and he's not afraid.'

Oskar stood a few metres from the bed; unsure what to do with himself, he watched her as she leaned over her father and saw the way they looked one another in the eye. 'You are not alone,' she whispered to him, in the very same mumbling way he'd heard her repeat to herself when she thought no one could see or hear her. Bo looked at her, maybe he blinked an extra time. She said it over and over. 'You are not alone, you are not alone.' It had an effect on Bo, that gentle chanting, it reached him, he raised his eyebrows and Oskar saw a sparkle in his eye.

And time passed more slowly, you could wander around inside the seconds now, and there would be some minor little reaction, Bo would cough, trying to expel mucus without success, try again – and then he was gone. He died with his gaze fixed on hers, with something that might have been a smile on his lips.

She didn't inherit a single krona from him, of course. He never had any money. She didn't get a single drop. Well, she did arrive home with a box a few days after Bo's death, full of his photo albums and a few old camera accessories. That evening she sat in bed surrounded by the lenses, sorting them and meticulously cleaning them, but after that he never saw them again. She must have chucked them. And the romanticising of him, which had already begun, it now gained speed. The bastard became a saint. The truth must never be uttered: that he had, for all her life, let her down. Because it was true, of course; he was never there, he never showed up. Bo was genuinely uninterested in Harriet for all those years; he didn't want to, or couldn't, forge a relationship with her, he was too broken. Their daily life, both hers and Oskar's, had taken place without Bo. They made a family, but their daughter hardly ever saw her grandfather. And even though he constantly disappointed Harriet, she never gave up hope. One time when Harriet and Yana were celebrating a birthday, Harriet had gotten hold of Bo and invited him to a birthday dinner. He'd made a vague promise to come. But he never showed up, and that evening Oskar watched as Harriet cleared away Bo's plate and silverware just before dinner, quickly and discreetly so no one would notice, trying not to let on how upset she was. It was her life's sorrow, wasn't it? The greatest betrayal she'd experienced. And yet, after his death a halo was placed above Bo's head, and Oskar couldn't stand it. One night he'd simply had enough of her falsifications. He protested, and they argued all night, shouting and wounding each other, and the lesson he'd taken from that incident was to never again discuss Bo with her, so that's how it was, that's how yet another topic was added to the list of things they never talked about.

Oskar and Harriet leave the bakery, the sun on their left. The grass along the little pedestrian mall is uncut, the flowers lean over the pavement and the air is so calm he can hear the bumblebees in them. Everything stands still; this town lacks circulation. She turns off on a narrow gravel path and he follows. They're in a forest, the sort of forest that immediately feels familiar, the sort of forest everyone carries with them. It's a Swedish forest full of pines and spruces, and the ground is damp. He can't take his eyes from the tall trees as they climb the hill, because they remind him of the woods in the archipelago. Suddenly a body of water emerges before him, a path of sunlight on its surface gleaming through the firs, and there's a yard with a mowed lawn. There's a low-slung white house facing the lake. Harriet walks straight across the lot. 'What if someone is home?' he says as he hurries to follow her.

'I don't give a shit,' she says.

They walk past a vegetable patch and she notices a trowel standing up in a bucket; she grabs it and heads for the lake. She stops by an apple tree growing next to a dock. 'Here,' she says. She looks around, then down at the ground in front of the tree. 'This is where Dad and I buried Bitty when I was little. And now we're going to dig up the grave.'

'Why?' he asks.

'There's something I want to show you.' She kneels down and thrusts the blade of the trowel into the soil. She takes a few scoops, depositing the soil in a pile, working faster now, each trowelful giving her fresh energy. She stops mid-motion, turns to Oskar. 'Feel this,' she says, and brings Oskar's hand to her chest. Through her shirt he can feel her heart beating wildly. 'That's how I want to die,' she says. 'An explosion.'

219

Chapter 20

Harriet

If there's a Doggy Heaven, there should also be a Bunny Heaven. Back when the family was a family, they had a dog. One summer afternoon it attacked a child, and a few weeks later the dog was gone. Dad sat on the edge of her bed that night and explained that the dog was in Doggy Heaven now. Maybe Dad was trying to comfort her, but really he was the one who needed comforting. Harriet thought a lot about Doggy Heaven after that. And now, as she digs a grave for Bitty alongside Dad, Harriet thinks that if there is a Doggy Heaven then there must also be one for rabbits. She tries to imagine what it would look like, but she can't.

'What are you thinking about?' Dad asks.

'Nothing,' she replies.

'You're always thinking about something.'

'I'm thinking about Bitty,' she tells him.

'Right,' Dad says. 'Good.'

One of the shovelfuls captures Dad's attention. There's old cow manure in the soil. He shows the pale brown dirt to Harriet and says there must have been a farm here a long time ago. He places a hand on one of the skinny branches of the apple tree, gently pinching one of the little leaves. 'This tree will grow nicely.'

When they're finished digging, Dad picks up the urn and holds it in his lap. The dirt from his fingers leaves black marks on the pale ceramic, and Harriet thinks it's too bad it's dirty now, but then she realises it doesn't matter. It will soon be totally covered in soil.

'I feel bad about something,' Harriet says. 'You said I could only give Bitty a tiny bit of chocolate, because his stomach couldn't handle candy. But he loved chocolate so much, remember? So sometimes I gave him more than I was supposed to, and then I was afraid he'd get sick.'

'But it turned out OK,' Dad says. 'He didn't get sick.'

'No, but one time Bitty was playing outside his cage and I had forgotten the chocolate bar on the floor, and he ate the whole thing.' Her voice catches in her throat. 'That whole night I was afraid he was going to die,' she says. 'And the next morning I was too scared to go over to his cage because I thought he would just be lying there.'

'So what happened?' Dad asked.

'Nothing. He was fine.'

'You see?' Dad says.

'I'm sorry I never told you,' she says.

'It's OK. It turned out fine.'

Harriet looks down at the ground, afraid to look up. To keep from crying she presses her tongue firmly to the roof of her mouth, that's what she usually does, and sometimes it works.

'Hey,' Dad says. 'Don't be sad. You gave Bitty an incredible meal. He got to eat a whole chocolate bar. It was the best day of his life.'

Harriet laughs and nods, and now she can look up at Dad.

'Should we bury the urn now?' he asks.

Harriet nods.

'It will be nice for him to reach his final resting place here on earth.'

'Then will he go to Bunny Heaven?'

'He's already there.'

'Is he?'

'Yes, he's somewhere up there.' Dad points straight up at the sky. 'He's running around in the sunshine in a meadow full of carrots.'

'Who will give him straw?' Harriet asks.

'There's straw everywhere. He sleeps under the stars, on a bed of dandelions, along with all his new bunny friends. In the morning they wake up and go hopping across the meadows.'

'I bet he likes that.'

'What we're doing now, burying him, this is only for us. So we can say goodbye.'

Harriet looks down. Holes are so scary when you can't see the bottom.

'Should we write a letter to send with Bitty to heaven?' Dad asks. 'We could each write one, and put them in the urn.'

'To who?'

'To whoever you want.'

Dad opens the camera bag. From one of its compartments he takes a notebook and two pens. He tears out two pages and gives one to Harriet. She kneels in the dirt.

'I'm going to write a letter to God,' she says.

'Good idea,' says Dad.

Harriet closes her eyes and feels the sun. She had always wondered what God looked like, but the only time she saw Him was in a dream. In that dream, she saw His face all across the sky. He was enormous. 'Is God watching us now?' Harriet asks.

'He's always watching us,' Dad replies. 'But He might be looking a little extra closely right now. It's great that you're going to write to Him.'

Harriet sits still, the paper in her lap, and maybe Dad notices her hesitation, because he rests a hand on her arm. 'Write whatever you want, just be honest. That's all God asks of you, for you to tell the truth.'

She sits there at the water's edge, the air is warm and the soil is cool, and all the sounds that had sounded far away before come closer and disappear. A rustle in the bushes, an animal that doesn't want to get in the way; swallows dart across the sky and hide under the roof of the small shed. A light breeze twists the pines, their trunks creaking softly. But then the world is quiet, it's just her and Dad at Bitty's grave, and she begins to write her letter to God.

'Dear God,' she writes, and then she stops, feeling lighter

than she had a moment ago. As though something has changed, but she can't say what. Like after a summer rain, when she goes outside and the air feels easier to breathe. That feeling she's so often had, of something heavy getting stuck inside her, just below her throat, a rock, maybe, and it weighs on her until it hurts all the way down to her feet, and it feels like her ribcage is about to collapse into her stomach. She takes a few breaths and realises she doesn't feel that way any more. She glances furtively up at her father, who's sitting next to her, bent over his empty sheet of paper. He's lost in thought. He hasn't written anything yet either, that's the kind of people they are, Dad and Harriet. They're alike, they take life pretty seriously, and now they're writing letters to God and they have to do it right.

'I love you, Dad,' she says.

Dad closes his eyes. He pinches the bridge of his nose and breathes heavily. For a moment it looks as though he's going to say something back; he opens his mouth, but nothing comes out.

Chapter 21

Yana

She digs and digs. Sometimes she thrusts the blade straight into a root and yelps with pain as the jolt goes through her hand. She listens to her own breathing. She leans the shovel against the trunk to rest for a while, looks up, the apple tree is larger than any she's ever seen. A few apples still dangle there, but most of them are on the ground around her, gleaming orbs everywhere. A gust of wind comes off the water and the odour of rot spreads across the lawn. Another gust. That lake is not healthy. She removes a few more shovelfuls but finds only soil, and if she hadn't seen the photograph of the exact location of the hole she would think she was digging in the wrong spot. But it's right here, by the dock, directly under the apple tree. In one of the last pictures in the album, her mother, as a girl, is sitting right here in front of a freshly dug grave, in low afternoon sunlight that makes her brown eyes glow mystically. The urn is in her arms, its lid open, and she's holding a scrap of paper up for the photograph. She has written something on the paper. It's impossible to tell what it says, but Yana knows that piece of paper is here in the earth right beneath her, and she is going to dig it up now.

Dad never wanted to talk about what happened that summer afternoon when Mom disappeared. He came home late that night. Yana had been waiting all afternoon and was sitting in the window seat in her room. Loser was on her lap and he sprang up and headed for the door, and a few seconds later she heard someone coming in. There stood Dad, and the first thing she said to him was, 'Where's Mom?' He went to the kitchen and sat at the dining table and pulled out a chair for her. Only once she was sitting across from him did she notice how haggard he looked, his eyes were elsewhere.

He embraced her and she sat there with her head buried in his chest, his body was shaking gently, like surges coming and going, maybe he was crying. She wasn't. She didn't cry even once.

Dad spent a lot of time in his room at first; she could hear him in the days that followed, loud, furious groans that penetrated the walls. And she thought only of Dad, and how he felt. She wanted to be there for him, and it wasn't until much later she realised how thoroughly he had betrayed her then. That initial silence, the selfish crying in his room, and the years that followed when he stopped talking to her. She moved out the year she was legally an adult, and Dad didn't object. He never got in touch, except for the dutiful phone calls each year on her birthday, full of empty congratulations. And they never mentioned Mom during those brief conversations, except for one time. It was on Yana's twenty-fifth birthday. Mom and Yana shared a birthday.

'It's a milestone birthday for Mom today,' Yana said.

'Yes,' Dad said.

'Happy birthday, Mom,' Yana said, and there was silence on the other end. His heavy breathing. He spoke with his mouth so close to the receiver and his silence was always so palpable, almost physical, his mouth, his teeth, his breath so close.

'Why haven't you told me more about Mom?' she asked.

'What do you mean?'

'About what happened that day?'

He said that Yana had been a little girl back then, and that you can't share just anything with a child. And reflexes from the past kicked in; Dad shouldn't have to carry this. His own grief is enough for him to deal with. But in the protracted silence that followed, something else took root. A feeling of defiance. 'But now I'm grown up,' Yana said. 'I want you to tell me.' She heard him breathing. She pictured him, memories from her childhood of Dad in the kitchen, talking on the phone, always bent over the rotary dial, so very close to it, as though the phone cord were awfully short.

He didn't tell her everything, and lots of it didn't make any sense, but he told her things she hadn't been aware of before. He told her that their destination had been a lake a few hundred metres away from the station. Mom had buried a pet there when she was little, and she'd also put a letter she'd written in the grave. They went there to dig it up, she wanted to show him the letter.

'What did the letter say?' Yana asked.

Dad's old phone crackled with some movement from the other end. He didn't remember, he said, he didn't want to talk about this any more.

Only when Dad died and she happened across the photo album did it all become clear to her. And now she's digging in a strange woman's yard, as though this were a matter of life or death, or *because* it's life or death, because she's opened herself up again. Yana allows herself to think about Mom, scraps of memories of her that open and close inside her, like heartbeats. She loved Mom. She remembers that so clearly now. She would have done anything for her, would have left it all behind if she'd asked her to. One Christmas Eve, the nativity scene started on fire. Mom turned around and dashed for the door, running for her life. Yana ran after her. When she reached the hall, Yana saw that Mom had taken a heavy blanket from a box, and she ran back to the living room. She threw the blanket over the fire and it went out right away. Everything was fine, but the memory comes back to her like a jolt, that impulse, the fact that she chose to abandon Dad with the fire and flee with Mom. But that was the way of it, Yana always chose Mom.

It was completely dark out now. No lights nearby, and the starry sky hanging low above her head. She digs and digs and soon she hits something hard and throws the shovel aside, sinks down on all fours, digs the rest of the way with her hands. The earth is damp and the smell of the lake is stronger now, and she sees the shape of the urn, dark and wet after decades in the ground, and she scrapes around it with her fingers, wiggling it and trying to pry it out by the lid, and at last it comes loose. It's bigger than it looks in the photos, and a lot heavier. Did that little girl carry this massive thing all by herself in her backpack? She carefully unscrews the lid and looks down into the black urn, reaches her hand inside and feels the ash between her fingers, it's still perfectly dry. And then she discovers something else in there, a scrap of paper. She grabs hold of it. There's very little writing on the paper, and so much ash that she can't read it. She turns on the torchlight on her iPhone and gently brushes it off. She reads the words, then reads them again, and slowly it dawns on her that something isn't right. Mom didn't write this note: this is an adult's handwriting. It must have been written by Mom's dad. She doesn't understand the brief text, doesn't get what it means. She feels around inside the urn again, searching for the other piece of paper, digging her hand ever more frantically through the ashes. She pours the contents on the ground in front of her and shines her torchlight on it but finds nothing but the charred remains of an animal. She feels inside the urn one last time, her fingers searching its walls. No note.

She puts down the urn. Leans against the tree.

She picks up the note that was written by the man who was her grandfather to see if there's anything else written on it. She checks the back, but there's nothing more, it's only this, only this little bit of writing, an almost fifty-year-old enigma.

'And I you, more than anything.'

Chapter 22

Oskar

Oskar looks up at the apple tree, its crooked branches; it's like a fairytale tree. An illustration from a biology book he'd had in school pops into his mind; they'd learned that a tree grows just as much below ground as above. He'd always disliked roots; when he was little his father had tasked him with pulling up the blackberry bushes in the garden each spring. Thorny thickets, the canes grown into each other, and most of the growth hidden thick below ground. If he pulled in one spot, the ground would heave five metres away. The bushes were alive – he yanked and they yanked right back – he let go and screeched in horror and disgust.

He watches her as she digs. She's sweaty, her thin blouse clinging to her skin; he can see her spine, two small muscles that run up the back of her neck. To keep from being blinded by a woman's beauty, you must imagine her skinned.

Harriet puts down the trowel and stands up, stretches her back. 'It's deep down,' she says.

'You know for sure this is where it should be?'

'Yes, definitely. It's here.' She pats her pockets and takes out the pack of cigarettes. She offers him one.

'Can't we just finish digging so we can be done with this?' he asks.

'Let's just have a cigarette,' she says.

They sit down to smoke, their backs against the apple tree. The air is perfectly still. A train approaches, passing by on the other side of the woods. Now he's there again, at her mercy, devoured by conditions she has set, stuck in an inescapable grasp. He's full of tiny reflexes he must constantly keep under control; he knows the signs, how his irritation grows. He knows the best thing would be to simply get up and walk away. He drags the half-smoked, glowing cigarette against the tree trunk and stands up, looks at Harriet. 'Time to dig,' he says.

'Can you take a turn?' she asks.

'Fine,' he says. And he kneels down and shovels soil into a pile beside the hole, and is surprised to find that there are different shades of colour, sometimes black and sometimes light brown.

'That's cow manure,' Harriet says, pointing.

'Oh, lovely,' Oskar replies.

Suddenly the trowel meets resistance, as though he's reached the bedrock, and Harriet kneels next to him. She scoops the soil away with her hands and they can make out the top of an urn. She uses her hands to dig around it and at last she gets it loose. 'This can't be,' she says softly. 'Here it is.' She gingerly unscrews the lid and sticks her whole hand inside. She brings up a flimsy piece of paper covered in ash and soot. 'This is what I wanted you to read.' She hands it to him and at first it looks like the paper is blank, but when he brushes off its dusty surface some text emerges, written in neat handwriting. He reads it, then reads it again. He hands it to Harriet, and she reads it too.

'You wrote this when you were little?' he asks.

'Yes.'

He takes the piece of paper back and looks at it. 'Why did you want me to see this?' he asks.

'Those words say as much about who I was then as who I am now.'

'Jesus Christ ...' he says. He stands up and brushes the dirt from his jeans. He takes a few steps towards the lake and gazes out, then whirls about to look at her. 'It always has to be about you, doesn't it?' he says.

She looks at him, a small crease appearing between her eyes.

'Everything you think about, everything you do and want to make other people do, it can only ever be about you, can't it? And even right now you don't see how maddening it is, this self-centredness, this boundless egoism. You have betrayed me, deceived me and our daughter, everything we have is falling apart, and you want me to go on a five-hour train trip to read a letter you wrote when you were a child.'

'It's not about me, it's about us; don't you get it? I want to explain to you why I'm not OK.'

'I don't want you to explain why you aren't OK!' he shouts. 'I want you to do something about it!' His vision contracts, he sees everything as if from a great distance, the dancing red spots come back, and they're so real he thinks they truly exist. 'Every time I wake up, I wonder, "How is she doing today? Is this a good day or a bad one?" You dictate the conditions of this family. When do you ever ask how I'm doing? Eventually I won't be able to handle it. No one can handle it, Harriet. I know you're depressed, that you're not OK, but in the end it's like there's nothing to do but smash it all to pieces.'

He holds up the piece of paper.

'And quit this stuff! All this looking backwards causes nothing but pain. I thought we were going to try to solve our problems, but once again, you just want to go back to some memory. But I'm here! You want to talk about why you wrote a letter to a rabbit when you were little, but you don't want to talk about why you slept with another man.'

She has stopped speaking, and at first all she wanted to do was interrupt him, but now she's just sitting there and gazing at the urn in her lap. She gets up, gives him a silent nod, turns around, and walks back up the hill.

'Are you just walking away right now?' he calls. 'Should I fill this hole in for you or do you want to just leave it here?'

She doesn't respond, continues up across the lawn.

'Harriet!' he cries. He watches her go, sees her stop at the fence. She places a hand on the top slat and leans against it for a while. Then she looks at the house, opens the gate, and walks straight for it. A few steps onto the deck, and she stands for a moment before the doors, looking in. Then she spits at the glass.

'What the hell,' Oskar mutters to himself. 'What the hell are you doing?' he shouts.

Harriet passes through the gate again, walks into the forest, towards the station.

Chapter 23

Harriet

The lake is a stew and the air is so still she can hear the creak of the gate opening by the house, and when she looks up Amelia is there, looking down at them. Harriet gets to her feet. 'Dad,' she whispers, and she taps his shoulder to make him look too. He's on his knees in front of the apple tree, scooping the last of the soil over the urn they've placed in the hole. He stands up as well.

When Harriet imagined what it would be like to see her sister again, she pictured them running towards one another, sharing a long hug. But, in fact, she can't take a single step, so she stays put, feeling foolish. Amelia comes down the hill, and Dad is the first one to reach her, embracing her eagerly.

'What are you doing here?' Amelia asks.

'We wanted to see you,' Dad says. 'Harriet wanted to see you.'

Their eyes meet and Harriet has to look away. Amelia comes a few steps closer.

'I'll take off for a little bit, so you two can chat,' Dad says. 'I'll go to the bakery by the station. I'll be back in an hour.'

Dad walks slowly up the hill, leaving the sisters behind with the silence. Harriet tries to think of something to say, a way to begin, but she doesn't know how.

'What happened to your hands?' Amelia asks, and Harriet looks down at her soil-covered fingers.

'I don't know,' she says.

'You don't know?' Amelia laughs. 'They're black.'

Harriet tries to brush the dirt away. 'I'm sorry for what I did,' she says. She still can't bring herself to look at her sister, her eyes are glued to the dirt on her skin, she rubs and wrings her hands. Amelia sits down next to the tree, and Harriet follows suit.

'What's done is done,' Amelia says, putting on a different voice.

Harriet laughs because she recognises an expression of their mother's, one she used often, and she can tell that Amelia is imitating her.

'No use dwelling on it,' Harriet moans in their mother's shrill tone.

'No use dwelling on it!' Amelia repeats.

They laugh together. And slowly a conversation takes shape. They sit by the apple tree, interrogating one another about the year that has passed, what they've been up to, polite little questions that receive polite little answers, and Harriet decides that Mom must have been right all along. What's done is done. She has to stop thinking about all the things she's done, and everything that has gone wrong. She should look forward instead, for the future is full of a thousand possibilities. She's with her sister again, and they can decide for themselves what will happen now.

'I was actually only stopping home for a minute,' Amelia says after a brief silence. 'I just had to pick up my riding clothes.'

Harriet doesn't understand what she means, or why she's telling her, but she nods and smiles at her sister.

Amelia looks at her watch. 'My lesson starts in twenty minutes,' she says.

'Oh!' Harriet says. 'You have to go?'

'Yeah.'

Harriet leaps to her feet, still smiling, feeling stupid for not understanding. Amelia gets up too, brushing dirt from her jeans.

'Maybe I could come along to your lesson,' Harriet says.

'That would be fun,' Amelia says. 'But they're really strict, not even parents can watch.' Amelia hugs Harriet. 'It's so silly,' she says. 'You've come so far.'

'It doesn't matter,' Harriet says.

'Take care of yourself.'

Amelia turns around and heads for the house. It happens so fast, and Harriet doesn't understand all of it right away. At first, what has happened burns just beneath her skin like a tiny bit of discomfort, something that probably isn't all that bad. She just feels a little embarrassed, that's all, like when you wipe a booger from your nose and someone notices. But as she stands there all alone, watching her sister walk up the hill, her anxiety expands and is soon perfectly evident. Her chest feels tight, her heart feels lashed up like a pork loin. She watches as Amelia enters the house and soon comes back out again, walks through the gate, takes the path through the forest. Anguish spreads through Harriet, a silent little panic. And she realises this is all familiar – she's felt like this once before. She watches her sister as she vanishes among the pines, and she sees no sign of the riding clothes Amelia said she needed to pick up. Harriet squeezes her eyes shut and she's no longer there by the lake, she's lying in her bed again and looking up at the ceiling, listening to Mom and Dad talking in the kitchen.

Chapter 24

Oskar

Oskar is still sitting by the tree. He screws the lid back on the urn and lowers it into the hole. He gently shovels dirt back over it. He feels his temples getting hot. Something tightens in his face, a grimace settling over it. He works faster, the cool soil against his fingers. He hears his pulse beating again. The smell of sludge driving off the lake once more. A few minutes ago, in the midst of the fighting and the rage, he wasn't there. Or, he was there, but he was only watching. He is the silent observer. He is there, he sees and hears everything but can't intervene. He takes it all in quietly, observing what the impulses do to him.

Later, once the rage has drained out of him, all that's left is destruction. The exchange of words settled in him, everything he said to Harriet gets sorted. Some of the worst things drive their teeth in even further. And he knows that another step has been taken, he has said some stuff that it's getting harder and harder to repair.

Is it possible to start over?

He has naïve dreams about it sometimes. Resetting the clock to zero. A few weeks ago, he had just shown a house in the archipelago to an older couple and was about to turn off the lights and lock up, but as he stood there all by himself on the stone steps, watching the glimmer of the sea between the tree trunks, he got the urge to go down to the shore. A narrow path, tiny pine cones rolling after him as he went, the dry ground, walking on fallen needles that crackled like a bonfire beneath his feet. He stood on the rocky shore, zipped up his jacket, and thought about her. Not of the weariness between them, or the fights, and he wasn't feeling weighed down by suspicion or hatred. He thought of everything they had once had together. He missed her, and he missed himself with her. Three fighter jets flew across the sky. It happened so fast, he just saw them zoom by like three black triangles low over his head, and then came the sound of them. He was so frightened that he fell to his hands and knees. When he got up again, he felt that something had changed, as though that bang had reset him. He was a blown-out husk. He had been given permission to start over. He ran up the rocky slope and got in the car, and he was full of such bright thoughts. But then he came home to the same apartment, the same irritation that soon exploded into something else. He doesn't remember what it was about that time, just that it all went to hell, with harsh words and that wild hatred that came out of nowhere, self-nourished, doubling every second. The silent observer appeared again, gloomily following the events from his place in the darkness.

Is it possible to start over?

Is it possible to find new ways to talk to Yana? Is it possible to look at Harriet again without all those layers of mistrust?

He is a monster.

He has filled in the hole again. The note Harriet wrote as a little girl is still on the ground, trembling in a breeze that can't quite manage to lift it. He stands up, brushes the dirt from his knees and walks up the hill. As he passes the white brick house, he stops short. The glass doors reflect the late-summer night, the glob of spittle gleaming in the low sunlight.

Chapter 25

Harriet

Harriet is once again sitting with her back to the fence, sitting and waiting for her father yet again as the hot afternoon sun moves across the treetops on the other side of the lake. Dad said he would be gone for an hour. She doesn't know how long she's been waiting, she hasn't quite learned to tell the time yet. She occupies herself with Dad's lenses, wiping them meticulously with a white handkerchief and placing them back in their compartments. At last Dad comes walking through the forest, along the path; he looks small among the tall trees.

Harriet aims the camera at him, observing Dad through the rectangle, it's like the colours are more vivid here, the foliage greener, the sky behind him bluer than it really is; it's like peering into a fairytale. She sees Dad walking through the forest, and he looks up and spots her and their eyes meet through the lens. She takes a picture. He comes up to her, takes the camera from her, inspects the settings. 'What were you taking a picture of?'

'For the photo album,' she replies.

'I see,' he says, making a few adjustments to the knobs on top of the camera. 'Your ISO is way too low, that picture's going to be awfully dark.' He puts the camera in the bag. 'Where's Amelia?' he asks.

'She had to go to her riding lesson,' Harriet replies.

'I see,' Dad says. He closes his eyes and presses his thumb and index finger to his eyelids. 'How was your talk?' he asks.

'It was OK.'

'Come on, let's go sit by the water for a minute.'

The dock is narrow and tilts a bit, there's bird poop around the iron posts where they come through the planks. Reeds grow on either side of the dock and they also stick up between the planks and tickle her shins as she walks to the end. Dad unties his shoes, takes off his socks, sits on the edge; he rolls up his trousers and dips his feet in the water. 'It's warm,' he says. 'Twenty-one degrees.'

Dad doesn't need a thermometer. He looks up at her and pats the spot next to him, and she settles there. She looks down at the water, at the sandy bottom that looks like mud, and tiny bubbles rise slowly to the surface. She sees a small school of fish swimming past their feet. They seem to move so slowly, as though they were passing through something thicker than water – syrup. A small cloud casts the dock in shadow and she looks up. The cloud up there is thin, the sun looks like a quickly rolling golden coin behind the white.

She doesn't want anything to do with the sun. Ever since her father told her it will go out someday, it makes her upset to think about it. Dad promised this would happen long after she was dead, but she worries anyway.

Dad elbows her in the side, and at first she thinks she's been discovered, that he knows what she's thinking about, but then he points out at the lake, and at first she doesn't see anything. 'See that big tree by the shore?'

'Yeah.'

'See the top of it?'

Now she notices the eagle sitting there. 'Whoa,' Harriet whispers. 'It's so big.'

'A white-tailed eagle,' Dad says. 'The biggest of all.'

She's never seen such a large bird. The lake is between them, yet she can clearly see its outline as it sits there grimly. Her heart beats faster.

'He's looking for something to eat,' Dad whispers. 'A fish swimming close to the surface. Or a fieldmouse in the trees. He's on the lookout.'

'No, I don't think so,' Harriet replies.

'You don't?'

'No,' Harriet says.

'Then what's he doing?'

'He's remembering.'

Dad makes a noise, she looks up at him and sees that he's smiling. The eagle is so still that it almost becomes one with the treetop. And then the creature spreads its wings and takes to the air. It flies low over the lake, heading right for them. Even Dad, who is never surprised by anything, sits up straighter on the dock as it approaches. Then it flaps its wings vigorously, and again. And again. And now it's carried on the wind way up high; without moving at all it floats on rare air, moving in wide circles right above them. Dad lies back on the dock and Harriet follows his lead. They look at the eagle, sometimes it flies right into the sun and she has to close her eyes. She sees its mustard-yellow claws, the size of human hands. Its wings so straight that they almost look man-made, the bird is a soaring brown rectangle against the blue, it reminds her of pictures she's seen of old fighter planes from the Second World War. It rises without moving a feather, sailing up to the limits of the atmosphere, becoming a dot that becomes a speck that vanishes into the blue. She turns her head, sees her father's face very close, he's still gazing up at the sky. His features look different now: is it because he's lying down? His face is smooth, evened out, his features softer. He turns to face Harriet and they look at one other for a moment without saying a word.

'I want to tell you now,' Harriet says. 'I want to tell you what Amelia said to me that time.'

Chapter 26

Yana

The cold has settled in for real now, the platform is white, ice crystals covering the asphalt and concrete. Red text scrolls across the digital information sign above her, a message that the train to Stockholm is delayed. She sits on the single bench at Malma Station and gazes out at the street that runs parallel to the tracks. There's a man with a dog, the animal is thoroughly inspecting a lamppost and the man doesn't try to stop him. A sound in the distance. She sees a bright headlight, a train approaching, and the scrolling information above her changes: 'Passing train.' The beam of light gets bigger, it's approaching fast and feels overwhelming, that such great power should be coming straight for her, and even though there's plenty of distance between her and the tracks she stands up and backs away a few steps, standing there paralysed as the train shoots by. Once it's gone, she approaches the tracks, looks down at the rails and the wet rocks.

The houses right across the street; from this elevated position, she can see straight into homes. She doesn't see any people, just dull colours striking the walls from various TVs. Yana hears a signal from another century, a sad little melody, three notes that remind her of the bell that called the pupils inside; it's her first day of school, she has a new backpack with white bunnies on it and doesn't want her father to leave.

And then comes the train that will take her home; it pulls into the station and its doors open reluctantly, and for a moment she just stands there wavering. No one gets on; no one gets off. A conductor in the far car steps onto the platform and stares at her without saying anything. She takes a step back, away from the train, showing him that she's changed her mind, she's not going to board the train. A whistle slices through the cold air, the door closes, and the train leaves the platform.

A new direction.

She walks towards the station building, out onto the little street with the ball-shaped streetlights that seem to float free in the air. She goes into the bakery, three candles flickering by the register; their wax has trickled down and hardened on the counter. A woman is bent over a table with a rag, rubbing at a food stain that doesn't seem to want to let go.

'Are you open?' Yana asks.

The woman straightens up and looks at the clock. 'We're closing soon,' she says. 'But you've got time.'

Yana orders a cup of coffee and takes a seat at the corner table right next to the window. The woman goes back to wiping the tables. Yana takes out the photo album, opens it on the first page, looks at the pictures that used to conceal a secret that would soon be uncovered, but which at this point are nothing more than rectangular mysteries. She looks at photo after photo. She observes the picture of her mother gazing out of the train window at the start of her journey with her father. Then she makes a discovery. She leans a little closer, realises that something is written on the back of the photo. She takes it by the edges, feels a slight resistance from the glue, and gently pulls it loose from the page. She turns the photo over and there are words there, in ink, written in a child's handwriting: 'You Are Not Alone.'

'Refill?' The woman from the cash register is suddenly right beside her, coffeepot in hand.

'Aren't you closing now?' Yana says.

'I can tell when someone needs a refill.' The woman pours her some more coffee. 'Did you miss the train?' she asks.

'Yeah,' Yana says. 'Missed it on purpose, you might say.'

The woman laughs. 'That's good,' she says, vanishing with her coffeepot. Yana returns her focus to the photo album, gently pulling the next picture loose, and the same thing is written on the back, but now it's there three times.

You Are Not Alone
You Are Not Alone
You Are Not Alone

On the back of each photo her mother has written the same

thing, again and again; on some of them it's written in tiny writing all over the white surface, and when she turns to the final picture, the one of her grandfather in front of a dark forest, she is so surprised she drops the photo and it flutters to the floor. She looks out of the window of the bakery, sees the dim lights of the platform at Malma Station. She closes her eyes, rests her forehead in her palm. She bends down to the side, looks at the photograph on the floor, sees what the little girl has written all over the back of the photograph, again and again, on every available space.

YANA
YANA
YANA

Chapter 27

Oskar

The sky is pink and the only hints of the sun are the tiny fires at the tops of the spruce trees. Oskar walks down the little hill through the forest and emerges onto the paved street that leads to Malma Station. He wanders past the great oaks and the white station building, up the stairs that lead to the platform. He looks around the platform and there, at the far end, on the old bench, he sees Harriet. She's put on her jacket, because it's cooler out now.

He walks towards her and soon she catches sight of him and stands up. They regard one another and a gust of wind ruffles her hair and she makes that gesture that belongs only to her, as she tucks the strands behind her ear and then places her palm over her cheek for a moment, as though she were pondering something. A memory of her, from their first night together in that chilly bar on Vasagatan, when a lock of hair fell down like that and she tucked it back, and as they looked at one another he couldn't maintain eye contact. When he approaches her, he takes her hand. 'I'm sorry,' he says.

At first she doesn't answer, her eyes fixed on the asphalt. 'Oskar,' she says. 'I slept with another man because I'm not in love with you any more.'

'I see,' he says.

She looks up at him and her eyes take on that shade he has never seen in any other eyes, as though the faint glow of lamps were inside them.

'You and I shouldn't be together,' she says.

He lets go of her hand. He hears three notes emanating from old loudspeakers, a chime that sounds oddly sad and reminds him of something he can't quite grasp. A school bell? A voice over the loudspeaker says that a train will be passing through without dropping off any passengers.

'This has to end,' she says. 'We can't do this to each other. We can't do this to Yana.'

'Yana,' Oskar says. 'After what you subjected her to at the pool, you have forfeited all right to tell me what's best for her. If we get a divorce, Yana stays with me.'

'We aren't going to fight over Yana,' Harriet says. 'She wouldn't want us to.'

'No, you don't get it.' He smiles at her. 'I talked to Yana yesterday. She's staying with me.'

She looks at him, that little crease between her eyes again.

'I asked Yana who she would want to live with if we got divorced,' Oskar says. 'She said she would want to live with me.'

Uncertainty spreads through her gaze.

'You have to respect that,' he says. 'She doesn't want to be with you.'

Now he sees the passing train behind her back, approaching at high speed from the valley and growing larger as it nears the platform.

'Did you make her say that?' she asks.

'I didn't make her do anything. This is what she wants.' He takes a step towards her. 'And it can't come as that much of a surprise to you. Don't you see the pattern?' He lowers his voice. 'Always the reject,' he says.

Harriet's mouth is half-open now.

'Rejected by your mother,' he says.

She brings her hands to her face, covering her eyes with her palms. 'No,' she says.

'Rejected by your sister,' he says.

'Stop, please.'

'Rejected by your father. And now, rejected by your only daughter.'

Harriet turns around and walks towards the tracks, stands at the very edge of the platform. The train grows behind her. She looks tentatively down at the rails, as though she were standing at a precipice.

'I can't do this any more!' Oskar calls. 'We're right back where we started. Yet another scene. Yet another chance to be the centre of attention.'

Harriet looks at the train, coming full-speed for the platform, a bell over by the dropping arm sounding in the wind.

'Who are you trying to fool?' he cries.

Harriet turns to Oskar, and he wants to shout something else at her but changes his mind. Something about her seems transformed. Something in her eyes, her facial features suddenly young. Harriet stands with her hands at her sides, her hair going every which way. She tries to smile, and when Oskar realises that she's fighting to hold back tears he suddenly recognises her: it's the girl from the photograph, the little kid on the bench with her father's camera bag burning over her shoulder and tears dancing just beneath her eyelids.

'No,' he mumbles.

Harriet turns to face the tracks, and just as the train enters the station, she jumps. A little leap, right in front of the speeding locomotive, and then she's gone.

The platform goes dark as the train hurtles over her, and then light again, the furious screech of the brakes on the other side of the station, and he falls to his knees. Anxious voices in the distance, quick steps on the platform, someone who saw what just happened. The bell at the dropping arm is still ringing. Otherwise, perfect silence has fallen over Malma Station. Oskar looks down, his forehead on the asphalt, and he sees nothing, but everything has a shape, the blackness is crystal clear, as perhaps it always is at that moment in life when you see yourself clearly.

Chapter 28

Harriet

'We were sitting here on the dock, right where we're sitting now,' Harriet says. She doesn't dare to look at Dad and stares at the lake instead. A reed is poking up right in front of her and she yanks it loose. The sludge on the bottom is stirred up; everything gets cloudy. Her feet disappear in the water, she looks legless. 'Amelia did the crab,' she says. 'Remember the crab?'

Dad laughs and nods. 'The crab,' he says simply.

'Then she told me she had something important she wanted to tell me,' Harriet says. 'Amelia said . . .'

Harriet stirs the bottom of the lake with the reed, poking it into the mud again and again. She squeezes her eyes shut, tries to say the words, but they get stuck in her throat.

'You can tell me,' Dad says. 'It's OK.'

'She said you're not my real dad.'

'I see,' Dad says. He looks up at the sky, closes his eyes.

He doesn't say anything for a few seconds. 'Where did she hear that?'

'She was eavesdropping on a conversation between Mom and her new boyfriend, and Mom said it. That I actually have a different dad.'

'I see,' Dad says again. He gazes out at the lake and makes a sound Harriet doesn't understand, a sudden gust of air from his nose, as though what he just heard has surprised him. He looks at Harriet again.

'I wanted ...' she says. She stops and tries to start over, focusing on it, because when she thinks of what she has to say she doesn't know if she will manage it without tears. 'I wanted to tell you but I was scared to,' she says. 'Because I'm so afraid it might be true.'

Dad places his hand over hers. The water grows still; for the first time she looks up at him.

'Have you been carrying that around for a whole year?'

She nods and tries to smile.

'That must have been awful,' he says.

'I think maybe there's something wrong with me, Dad.'

'There's nothing wrong with you.'

'Yes there is. Sometimes I feel like the world is going to disappear. I get scared to look around because I'm afraid that what I was just looking at will be gone. And sometimes it's the other way around, I have to look around, and spin around and look at everything, to find proof.'

'Proof of what?' Dad asks.

'That I exist.'

The wood is warm, the planks hot after a day in the sun.

'When Mom and Amelia disappeared I was scared,' she says. 'And that's why you have to still be here, because if you're gone, then maybe everything will disappear.'

'I'm still here,' Dad mumbles.

'There has to be someone who will always be here. That's why it's so important that you exist. It's really important, Dad.'

'I do exist,' Dad says softly. 'Listen to me. It doesn't matter what anyone else says. You are my daughter. I am your father. And I'm not going anywhere.'

She nods. Dad looks down at the water; he's illuminated from below by the sun's reflection on the surface, his face gleams, it looks like he's gazing down at a pile of gold. He catches sight of a reed of his own and pulls it up. He lays his reed across hers.

'Is it true?' Harriet asks.

'Is what true?'

'What Amelia said.'

Dad takes a deep breath, holds it in his lungs for a moment, then lets it out. 'All I've ever believed is that you are my daughter and I am your father,' he says. 'Because we're so similar. We both love meatballs, but we both pick off the lingonberries.'

She laughs.

'We both like everything of beauty,' he says. 'You've got your drawings and I've got my photography. We see pictures everywhere. And I think we're both sad sometimes because we feel like something's missing. We want to be free, you and me, and at the same time we're afraid of being alone. Right?' Dad looks at her, a quick examination. 'Listen,' he says, his voice gentle and his hand on her back. 'Don't cry, sweetie.' His large, soil-covered thumb wipes Harriet's cheek. 'There, sweetie,' he says. 'I'm going to show you something.' He rolls up his sleeve and shows her his shoulder. There's his tattoo, the four words that have seeped out into his skin, the brief sentence she's wondered about so often, has tried to make sense of when she thinks he isn't looking. 'Do you see this tattoo?' He presses just beneath it so the skin is drawn out and now she can read the words. 'Do you see what it says?' he asks.

'Is it in English?'

'Yes. "You are not alone." It's from a song. I listened to it over and over. It was like he was singing just for me. He tells me I shouldn't be afraid, that I'm not alone. And he says . . . ' Dad stops and closes his eyes. 'He says I'm wonderful. No one had ever told me that before.'

He takes her hand and tells her to close her eyes and she does as he says. She feels the sun on her face and a light breeze on her forehead. 'Every time you feel like the world is shifting, when you feel scared or worried, you should do this,' he says. 'Repeat after me. "You are not alone."'

'You are not alone,' she says.

He says it once more, and she repeats it. She says it again and again and sometimes she hears her father saying it, *you are not alone*, his strained voice sounding like it's far away, in a different reality. And Dad puts his arm around her, he's so big, and when he hugs her he is everywhere. 'You are my daughter. I know it's true, because I can feel it all through my body, all the time. Do you understand?'

She nods.

'And I don't know if what your sister said is true. It doesn't matter to me. But do you want to know?'

'No.'

He tucks her head against his chest. She feels his breath, a tiny warm gust on her hair.

'If you want to, we can find out.'

'No, I don't want to know,' she says. 'I just want you to stay here.'

'I'm here,' Dad says. 'I'll always be here.'

Thanks

The characters in this book are evidently book lovers and have been inspired by other authors. Harriet's thoughts about seeing oneself clearly once in a lifetime are something she must have read in a poem by Pablo Neruda, because that sentence is reminiscent of something he wrote. When she tells Oskar about the most beautiful sentence she's read in a book, she cites one from Jonathan Safran Foer's *Extremely Loud & Incredibly Close*.

This book was written between late autumn of 2020 and the summer of 2022. As I worked I received invaluable help from many people, and I'd like to thank them here.

Thanks to Daniel Sandström at Albert Bonnier Förlag, without you this book would have been seventeen per cent worse. I'd also like to thank Åsa Beckman, who was an ever-present reader as I wrote — I've never encountered anyone with the same feeling for what isn't true or what lacks melody in a piece.

Thanks, too, to editor Lotta Bergqvist at Bonniers and Åsa Ernflo, who did intense work with this book in its last stages.

Thanks to Detective Inspector Jonas Lindberg and physician Olle Wallner.

I've also had friends and colleagues who read and provided valuable thoughts. Thanks to Josefine Sundström, Fredrik Backman, Fredrik Wikingsson, Ruben Östlund, Ninni Schulman, Klas Lindberg, Calle Schulman, Sigge Eklund, Ivar Arpi, Veronica Zacco, Eric Rosén and Pascal Engman.

I'd also like to thank Astri Ahlander at Ahlander Agency, who is not only the agent who's managed to sell my books abroad but also one of the most important figures when it comes to working on the text itself.

Finally, and most of all, I'd like to thank my wife Amanda, always my first and last reader.

Alex Schulman